MISSED CONCEPTION

What Reviewers Say About Joy Argento's Work

Exes and O's

"I really appreciated the new take on a burned lover in Ali. Instead of pushing love away forever, she decides to actively seek out what has gone wrong in order to do better in her future. I also enjoyed how the story focuses on what a healthy relationship should be and how to get to that. It was refreshing. ...If you're in the mood for a gentle second-chance romance that has just enough angst, great character development, and will have you dying for a donut, run for this book!"—*Lesbian Review*

Before Now

"*Before Now* by Joy Argento is a mixture of modern day romance and historical fiction. ...There was some welcome humour and a bit of angst. An interesting story well told."—*Kitty Kat's Book Review Blog*

Emily's Art and Soul

"...the leads are well rounded and credible. As a 'friends to lovers' romance the author skillfully transforms their budding friendship to an increasing intimacy. Mindy, Emily's Down syndrome sister, is a great secondary character, very realistic in her traits and interactions with other people. Her fresh outlook on life and her 'best friend' declarations help to keep the upbeat tone."—*LezReviewBooks*

"This was such a sweet book. Great story that would be perfect as a holiday read. The plot was fun and the pace really good. The protagonists were enjoyable and Emily's character was well fleshed out. ...This is the first book I've read by Joy Argento and it won't be the last. I'm looking forward to what comes next." —*Rainbow Literary Society*

Visit us at www.boldstrokesbooks.com

By the Author

MISSED CONCEPTION

by

Joy Argento

2022

CREDITS
EDITOR: CINDY CRESAP
PRODUCTION DESIGN: SUSAN RAMUNDO
COVER DESIGN BY JOY ARGENTO AND TAMMY SEIDICK

Acknowledgments

Special thanks to Olessia Butenko and Tobie Hewitt for finding all the mistakes that I miss. I am so grateful for you. Thank you to my support system, without whom I would probably curl up in a ball and suck my thumb.

Kate Klansky
Susan Carmen-Duffy
Karin Cole
Georgia Beers
Barbara DiFiore
And my kids, Jamie, Jess, and Tony

Dedication

For Kai

Chapter One

Is this how I do it?" Hannah Kennedy asked her daughter. Now that Cassidy was eighteen there was no reason not to let her have her way on this. She had been bugging Hannah for the last two years to send their DNA into one of those ancestor sites, Genetic Experts, so Cassidy could see exactly which traits she had gotten from her sperm donor father and which came from Hannah.

Her dark hair, brown eyes, and olive completion didn't match Hannah's looks. Nor did they match the donor's information. Hannah and her wife, Teri, chose a donor who closely matched Teri's characteristics, light blond hair, green eyes, fair skin, and more cerebral than athletic.

The plan was for Hannah to carry the baby and have the baby share both of their looks and easygoing personalities. The plan never included Teri dying in a car accident when Cassidy was only two and Hannah raising her by herself.

"You're fifty years old, Mom. How can you not figure out how to spit into a tube?"

Hannah tried not to let Cassidy's intense personality get under her skin. "I'm only forty-two, and I just want to make sure I'm doing it right. Are you done with yours?"

Cassidy held up the tube, clearly filled to the line.

"What if I run out of spit?"

"Mom!" Eye roll.

"Lighten up. I'm just teasing you. I'm done." She held it up.

Cassidy handed her one of the plastic bags that came in the kits and read the directions from the pamphlet that was enclosed. "Place your full tube in the plastic bag, remove the blue strip, and seal the bag closed." She glanced at Hannah. "Did you put the cover on the tube?"

"No, Cassidy. I thought it would be a good idea to let my spit spill out into the bag."

Being a single parent wasn't easy, not that there weren't plenty of good times, but Hannah didn't like it when Cassidy treated her like she was an idiot. She regretted her words and tone as soon as they were out of her mouth.

"Yes, honey," Hannah said. "I put the cap on. I have it sealed in the bag. I'm ready for the next step."

"Okay. I'm going to register them." Cassidy pulled the laptop, already opened to the site, across the table. "Ancestry report. Check. Get a list of DNA relatives. Check. Permission to be added to family trees—blah, blah, blah. Check," Cassidy said, more to herself than to Hannah.

"We've got our registration numbers on our cards. Put your card and vial in the box, seal, and drop in a mailbox."

Hannah followed the directions and handed the box to Cassidy. "Want to drop this in the mailbox on your way to work?"

Cassidy started taking horseback riding lessons at Horizon Stables when she was thirteen. She was good enough that she now taught the younger kids there. She often worked around the barn and helped with the horses to earn extra pocket money and to pay for her car insurance. That had been the deal when Cassidy decided to go to the local community college—Hannah would buy her a late model used car and Cassidy would be responsible for the upkeep and insurance.

Her love of horses translated to her majoring in equine studies with an eye toward training horses. Although she hadn't ruled out veterinary school in the future. She just wasn't sure she wanted to put that much time or money into schooling.

Hannah and Teri had started saving for her college fund when she was a baby, and Hannah managed to put a good chunk of money aside from Teri's life insurance toward it. It would cover her four years of college for her bachelor's degree, but if Cassidy did plan on going to veterinary school after that, they would just have to rely on student loans for it.

She was surprised but grateful when Cassidy opted for the community college and staying at home for at least a year, maybe two. Hannah wasn't looking forward to the time Cassidy moved on to a four-year college, possibly—probably—out of state.

It'd been just the two of them for so long. Of course, Hannah had her mom and her two sisters, and both she and Cassidy had friends, but it had felt like the two of them against the world for so long. Hannah had dated here and there in the years after Teri died, but everyone paled in comparison and she had Cassidy and a business to worry about. That took up most of her time and attention.

"Can you write the return address on these?" Cassidy asked, bringing Hannah out of her thoughts.

"Sure."

"By the way, it's family day at Horizon Stables on Sunday. I thought it would be nice if you came by and watched me work with the kids."

"This Sunday?" Only two days away. "That's not much notice. I'll have to cancel dinner with Grandma."

"Ask Grandma to come. She never comes to family day."

Hannah's mother was not a fan of horses. And for that matter, Hannah wasn't either, but she did her best to support Cassidy's interests. Truth be told, horses scared Hannah. She knew it was an unreasonable fear, but knowing that didn't do anything to stop it. It didn't seem to matter how many times Cassidy told her how gentle they were. So she kept her distance.

Hannah handed the boxes, complete with return addresses, to Cassidy. "I'll ask. But you know she has the rest of the family coming over too." It had become a tradition to have dinner on Sundays at her mom's house. It seemed even more important to her mom since her father had died three years ago.

"Invite them all. Maybe we can all do dinner at Grandma's or even our house afterward."

Horses were important to Cassidy, but so was family. No one except Hannah had taken much interest in family day at the stable, and Hannah knew that bothered Cassidy. "I'll see what I can do."

"Thanks, Mom." Cassidy slipped the DNA tests into her backpack. "I'm going to help Denise with the new horse later, so I won't be home for supper." With that she was out the door and gone.

Great. Another night of eating alone. It wasn't worth cooking for just one, and Cassidy rarely ate more than a snack when she got home from the stable. Looked like a Chinese food in front of the TV kind of night. Oh well, there was a movie on Netflix she had wanted to watch anyway.

The older Cassidy got the more time Hannah seemed to spend alone. It was to be expected, she reasoned. Most of Hannah's friends were married and busy with younger kids to look after, as was her sister Linda. She was close to her sister Sarah, but Sarah usually had dinner at home with her husband. They didn't have a lot of time for Hannah.

Petals of Love, the flower shop she'd started with Teri over twenty years ago, kept her busy of course, but work was not life. She needed to get a life. Maybe she'd take a class or something.

Her food was delivered in record time, and she transferred it from the paper cartons to a plate, poured herself a glass of wine, and settled down on the couch.

"It doesn't get any more exciting than this," she said to the fried rice. "Yeah. I need to get a life." She just wasn't sure where to look for one.

CHAPTER TWO

Maggie Walsh pulled her hair into a ponytail. With its current length, it was the only thing she could do with it. When she rode the horse with her hair down, it whipped across her face, which didn't make for a pleasant time. Clover, her favorite of the four horses in her stable, was a beautiful white Thoroughbred. His gentle disposition made him the perfect horse, not only for Maggie to ride but also for students who were taking more advanced riding and jumping lessons.

"God, I wish I had your tan," Randi said as Maggie approached the barn. Randi had worked for her for the last five years. Maggie didn't know what she would do without her. As the saying went, it was hard to find good help, and Maggie had found that to be the case trying to find people to muck the stalls, groom the horses, and help with riding lessons. Randi had become her right-hand man. Maggie hated that term, but right-hand woman sounded weird.

"Get your butt out of the barn once in a while and maybe you can have one too." Maggie smiled at her.

"My boss is too much of a hard-ass. She refuses to even let me see the sun, let alone spend any time in it," Randi teased her.

"Yeah. Bosses can be real dicks sometime. Why don't you saddle up Jake after you get Clover ready and you can go riding with me? But I would put some sunscreen on that pale skin of yours. You're going to burn like a son of a gun if you don't."

It was something Maggie knew she didn't need to tell Randi. Her red hair and freckled skin drew the sun rays to her like a magnet. Not only would Randi generously apply sunscreen, she would have on a long-sleeved shirt and hat, despite the summer heat.

"I thought you had a lesson with Jake this afternoon," Randi said. Jake was her American paint horse. With his perfect patchwork of brown and white hair, he could have been used as a model for *Horse Rider* magazine.

"They canceled. So, he's all yours if you want to go with me. I need to check out trail three. After yesterday's storm I need to see if any branches came down. Thought it might need to be cleaned up."

"I'll grab my gloves. I can go do it if you want."

"I didn't ask you to come along so you can work. I asked you to come for the company. I'm more than happy to do it myself. If you feel like helping, great. If not, you don't have to."

Randi had become more than just a hired hand. She had become a friend. And for that, Maggie was grateful.

"You need to get yourself a girlfriend to go riding with you. Not that I'm not happy to do it. I just hate thinking of you going home to that empty house every night."

That empty house was only a hundred yards from the barn, and while Randi was right, it was empty except for her, she wasn't lonely in it. Sure, she'd had a few relationships, but none of them had worked out. She was just fine being alone. She didn't need anyone to complete her. She was complete and fine all by herself. "Not this again. Just because you found the love of your life, doesn't mean that fate is destined for everyone."

Randi looked up at Maggie and squinted against the sun. "Just because you haven't had any luck in love so far doesn't mean you can't find it. You're only forty-eight years old. Still plenty of life left. And you're gorgeous. Hell, if I leaned that way you would be at the top of my list."

As much as Maggie appreciated the compliment, she didn't appreciate the conversation. She heard it often enough from her sister; she didn't need to hear it from anyone else. "I'm going to go do some paperwork. Let me know when you have the horses ready to go." She headed toward the house.

"Way to ignore the obvious," Randi called after her.

Maggie raised a hand, indicating that she heard her, but was done with the conversation. She didn't know why people in relationships wanted everyone else to be in a relationship too.

She had a full life. Full enough, anyway. Sure, it would be nice to have someone to cuddle up to at night. She had that on occasion. She wasn't a monk—or whatever the female version of that was. But they were never much more than one-night stands. Why invest your heart when it was bound to get broken in the end? She'd done that once. Granted it wasn't a romantic relationship she had been banking on, but it broke her heart nonetheless. It nearly broke her bank account as well. Yeah, best to be alone and accept your lot in life.

Ready, boss!

Randi's text came through just as Maggie finished paying the bills for the month. Money could get tight in the winter, but business was booming during the rest of the year. Giving riding lessons, renting out horses to experienced riders, and boarding horses brought in enough money to keep Rocking Horse Stables in business and provide paychecks for one part-time employee and Randi.

Be right there.

Maggie grabbed her cowboy hat on the way out the door and slipped it on her head. She didn't think she looked particularly chic in it, but it certainly helped to keep the sun off her face.

Randi had both horses by the side of the barn, near the path that led to one of three riding trails on the property. She had a hold on the reins even though neither horse was likely to wander away.

Maggie slipped her foot into the stirrup, grabbed the far edge of the saddle, swung her leg over the horse's rump, and settled comfortably down. Her five-foot, nine-inch height definitely helped with the process. Randi, a good four inches shorter used a mounting block, not that she couldn't get on the horse without one, but it was easier on Jake's back that way.

Careful to keep a bit of slack in the reins, she set off at a slow pace, Randi following behind. She didn't want to open Clover up to a canter or even a trot until she was sure the trail ahead was clear. She'd already checked trails one and two and found some small debris. Trail three had more trees lining its edges. She would be surprised if they didn't find some sizable branches across it.

Just as she suspected, they found no less than six large branches and more than a dozen smaller ones on the trail. Satisfied that they had them all, they headed back to the barn at a trot.

Maggie let the light breeze sail over her and wash her troubles away. Not that she had many. She lived a simple life. A life that she hadn't planned on living alone, but fate had other plans for her. The hurt from over eighteen years ago still lingered in her heart. The hole it left could never be filled and she had stopped trying years ago.

She had accepted her lot in life. It was what it was, as they say—a good life—with a huge void.

CHAPTER THREE

Hannah couldn't help but smile at Cassidy's excitement. It had been four weeks since they'd sent their DNA to Genetic Experts and the results were finally in. Cassidy had gone so far as to create a spreadsheet with characteristics, eye color, hair color, and such, as well as ancestry composition, so she could chart out what had come from Hannah and what would have undoubtedly come from the sperm donor.

"Ready?" Cassidy asked her.

"As I'll ever be." They sat at the kitchen table with Hannah's laptop between them. It wasn't a huge kitchen, but it fit nicely into their two-story house. It was mostly just the two of them for meals; they didn't need it to be much bigger. And Hannah usually ate in the living room when she ate alone, which seemed to be more and more often these days.

Cassidy clicked on the email from Genetics Experts and then clicked on the link to bring her to her results. She went to the ancestry report first. "I thought you said you were mostly Swedish and Irish," Cassidy said.

"I am."

Cassidy scrunched up her face and bit her bottom lip.

"What?" Hannah asked.

"It doesn't list either of those in my results." More lip biting.

"That's weird. What does it say?"

"It says Italian, thirty-eight percent. Greek, thirty-four percent and then a little each of some other things."

Hannah turned the computer so she could see it better. Sure enough, that's what Cassidy's results said. That didn't make any sense. Either the results were wrong, or she had been given misinformation on her nationalities her whole life.

"Huh. That's strange. My grandmother came over from Ireland when she was sixteen. "How come it says zero percent Irish? This can't be right." She positioned the computer in front of Cassidy again. "What does mine say?"

A few clicks later, Cassidy had Hannah's information in front of them. It listed Irish at forty-five percent and Swedish at thirty-nine percent. "See, I'm Irish and Swedish. Yours must be wrong. They must have switched it with someone else's."

"Crap. What are we supposed to do now?" Cassidy asked, her frustration obvious.

Hannah scrolled down to the bottom of the page. "There's a chat box here. Let's ask them. Do you want me to do it?" Hopefully, they could figure this out.

"Go for it."

Hannah typed. *We just got our results from your company and my daughter's must be wrong. Can you check to see if it got mixed up with someone else? Please.*

The representative responded. *It would be a first if it did get mixed up with someone else. But I would be happy to help you with that. May I have your daughter's name and the reference number on the kit she used?*

Cassidy had taken a picture of the reference number and read it off to her. Hannah typed it in, along with Cassidy's full name.

Representative: *That matches our records. The information you received were the results of the sample we got with that reference number on it.*

Hannah: *That can't be right.*

Representative: *We can send you another kit free of charge if you would like to repeat the test.*

Hannah: *Yes. Do that please, because there is no way these results are correct.*

Hannah verified the address with the representative and ended the chat.

"No sense looking at the rest of it if it isn't even my information," Cassidy said. "Damn it."

"I'm sorry, honey. We'll get it straightened out." At least Hannah hoped they would.

❖

The representative must have put a rush on the kit because it showed up in the mail two days later. There was a sticker in the box that said TEST UPON ARRIVAL for them to put on the box that they mailed back with the new saliva sample.

The email with the new results showed up in Cassidy's inbox a week after they sent it back. They were exactly the same as the first sample.

"I don't get it," Cassidy said. She clicked on the tab that said DNA Relatives. "Mom, this is so off. How can they mess it up so bad?"

"What are you seeing?" Hannah asked her.

"It has relatives on here who I don't even know. Look. It doesn't even have you listed as my mother."

Hannah stared in disbelief. No. She wasn't listed as Cassidy's mother. But someone else was. There were two first cousins listed, as well as a slew of second to sixth cousins. No one on the list was familiar to Hannah.

She clicked over to her own results. Cassidy wasn't listed as her daughter. It did, however, list Sarah as her sister, one of her cousins, and other, more distant relatives. It wasn't possible that they had messed up Cassidy's test twice. Was it?

"This sucks. Is yours right? Do they have your relatives listed?" Cassidy asked.

"Yes. Mine is right." Hannah's brain was swirling. She found it hard to hang on to any one thought for more than a few seconds. What did this mean? Who was the woman listed as Cassidy's mother? Was it possible Cassidy wasn't her daughter? That was just ridiculous. Of course, she was her daughter. She looked just like—no—she didn't look just like—anyone in Hannah's family. She didn't look like the description of the sperm donor either. No. Stop. This wasn't making any sense.

"Mom? What's going on?"

Cassidy's question brought her out of her thoughts. "Um. They must have screwed up. Maybe someone has the same name as you or something." No sense panicking Cassidy. Hannah was doing enough panicking for them both. She'd heard of babies being switched at birth, but they had safeguards against that now. Besides, Cassidy was never out of Teri's or her sight from the time she was born until they took her home from the hospital. The DNA lab had to be wrong. What other possible explanation could there be?

Maggie scrolled through her emails. Most were junk mail that didn't make it to her spam folder. She shook her head. How the hell did all these companies get her private email address anyway? You sign up for one newsletter and all of a sudden your email is full of crap.

She clicked on an email from Holly's Horse Supplies and scrolled through their list of specials, not that she needed anything, but it never hurt to see if there were any bargains she couldn't pass up.

A little farther down was an email from Genetic Experts announcing that she had new DNA relatives. She followed the link to the list. She had originally sent in her DNA to see if her mother, who took off when she was only three, had also sent her DNA in. She knew it was a long shot and had long ago given up. But every once in a while, when she got an email like this, her heart rate picked up and her breathing became shallow, and every time, without fail it was some other relative. More than likely some distant cousin. Her sister Jean's daughters showed up on the list, but those were the closest relatives she'd ever had listed.

She swallowed hard and clicked on the link. It wasn't her mother. Something deep inside her told her it wouldn't be. But what it was took her breath away. It listed someone named Cassidy Kennedy as having fifty percent shared DNA. Daughter.

What? Maggie didn't have a daughter, or any kids for that matter. She had tried many years ago, but the IVF procedure had failed. Two eggs retrieved. Two fertilized eggs implanted. Two eggs failed to thrive. No babies. No daughter.

This had to be some kind of mistake.

Chapter Four

W hat do you think it means?" Hannah's sister Sarah asked her.

The light breeze felt good against Hannah's skin. But her face felt hot with emotions. The outdoor seating at Middletown Café was filling up fast. She sipped her tea before answering. "I can't imagine they messed up the tests twice."

Sarah flipped a lock of blond hair over her shoulder. "Maybe you should run it again with a different company. There are a bunch that do that DNA stuff."

"What it if it says the same thing?"

Sarah squinted her eyes. "What aren't you telling me, Hannah?"

"Huh?" Hannah wasn't sure she wanted to say the words that had been swirling in her head out loud. It might make them real.

"I can tell you have something going on inside that brain of yours. It's got you all kinds of worried. Do you think that somehow Cassidy isn't your biological child?"

That was exactly what Hannah had been thinking. She knew without a doubt that the baby she gave birth to was Cassidy. But what if the embryo they implanted wasn't hers? "Yeah," was her simple answer.

"How would that even be possible?" she asked, her voice soft. Concern showed in her deep blue eyes.

"What if they mixed up the embryos at the fertility clinic? It wouldn't be the first time. I've read about other cases where that happened."

Sarah set her coffee cup down, reached across the table, and placed her hand over Hannah's. The warmth was comforting but not comforting enough to stop the sour taste rising up Hannah's throat.

"You may be jumping to conclusions and getting yourself worked up over nothing. The chances of that are very slim," Sarah said.

"Slim isn't impossible." Hannah knew her sister was right. She needed to calm down, but she had a bad feeling about this. She couldn't seem to shake it. "I mean look at Cassidy. She doesn't look like anyone else in the family. She certainly doesn't look like me. And she's so tall compared to the rest of us."

"Don't you take that chance when you use a sperm donor? Maybe she looks like him."

"We got to pick the donor and choose the characteristics we wanted. She doesn't match that either."

Sarah sat back and took a sip of her coffee.

Hannah could only imagine that it was as cold as her tea had gotten. They were doing more talking than drinking.

"How do you know the donor told the truth?"

"We did our research. They vet those guys. It isn't just some Joe that walks in off the street and jerks off into a cup."

Sarah spit out a mouthful of coffee. Thankfully, she turned her head away from Hannah before doing it. A bit of coffee dribbled down her chin and she caught it with a napkin. "I'm glad you can make light of it."

Light wasn't what Hannah was feeling at that moment. "It's either joke about it or scream, and right now it's all I can do to keep from screaming."

"Hannah, Cassidy is your kid no matter what, matching DNA or not. Nothing is going to change that."

"But this involves more than just Cassidy and me." She swallowed back the lump that was forming in her throat and held back the tears that were threatening to make an appearance.

"What do you mean?"

"There's a woman out there who, more than likely, got notified by Genetic Experts that she has a new DNA relative registered with them. One click of the mouse and she is going to be told that she has a daughter—a daughter who she didn't know existed. I don't think it's something she is going to ignore. I wouldn't."

"Oh shit. I never thought of that. By the same token, if there was a mix-up with the embryos, do you think it's possible that she was implanted with your kid?" Sarah seemed to think for a moment. "Sorry. That sounded crass. Not sure how to phrase the question."

That was a possibility Hannah had considered. If there was a biological child out there from her embryo, would she want to know him or her? It wasn't like they could just exchange kids and go on with their lives. "I don't know. I don't know anything anymore. I feel like my safe little world has come crashing down around me."

"How is Cassidy feeling about all this?"

"Oh my God, I didn't tell her what I suspect. She thinks the results they posted are wrong. I'm going to let her think that until I know something for sure."

"And how are you going to know for sure?"

"I've actually thought about contacting the woman listed as Cassidy's mother. But on the off chance that she didn't see the new relative…" Hannah made quotation marks with her fingers. "I don't want to tell her. I'm thinking my only other option is to contact the fertility clinic."

"Do you really think they would tell you if they screwed up? They might not even know."

"Yeah, I've considered that." And about every other possible way she could get at the truth. "I am at a loss for what else to do."

"How about a private detective? Harold knows a guy who does that kind of work. I think he's done some stuff for the company Harold works for." Harold, Sarah's husband, was a decent enough guy, although Sarah did complain about him from time to time. But what wife didn't have gripes about her husband?

"What would that tell us?" That was one option Hannah hadn't considered.

"He could investigate the other woman," she said, making her sound more like a mistress than the possible birth mother of Hannah's only child.

"And find out what?" Just the thought of it made Hannah's stomach clench.

"If she used the same fertility clinic around the same time you did."

That made sense. If she hadn't used the same clinic in the same time frame Hannah and Teri did, that would rule out the possibility of an embryo switch. And if she did—that was too much for Hannah's heart to take. Her brain on the other hand decided to ruminate on that theory continually.

"Hannah, what do you think? Should I get the PI's info?"

Hannah couldn't help but laugh, despite her anxiety. Or maybe it was because of it. "The PI's info? We sound like we're in a crime novel. Let me think about it for a while."

"You realize you may be freaking out for nothing, don't you? There's no proof that there was a mix-up. It really could just be a computer mistake on the part of the Genetics Experts."

Hannah was hoping that was the case, but she was far from convinced.

❖

"Great job today, Nikki," Maggie said to the young riding student. "Don't worry about brushing Milkshake down. I'll do it later." They'd already walked him around the ring a couple of times to cool him down. Maggie had had trouble focusing on teaching and she had almost canceled. Her mind continually returned to the email from Genetics Experts the day before and the fact that it claimed she had a daughter. She let Milkshake loose to wander in the paddock and walked Nikki over to where her mother was waiting. They exchanged pleasantries and Maggie waited until they drove away before heading inside the house.

It seemed to take forever for her computer to fire up, and Maggie tapped her fingers impatiently on the desk. She looked one more time at the list of relatives on the Genetics Experts site, just to make sure she had really seen what she thought she had. It said the same thing it had the day before. Daughter. Cassidy Kennedy.

A search on Facebook revealed more than thirty Cassidy Kennedys. She scrolled back up to the top of the list and examined each picture and any personal information listed, especially birth years or any other dates giving an indication of the person's age.

She was about halfway through the list when she came across the profile picture of a young woman standing by a horse. "That would be too much of a coincidence," she said to herself. "Let's see what we've got here." The birthday listed was June 24, but there was no year.

She couldn't see much more than a profile picture and a few memes on her page. It must be set to private, she reasoned. She clicked on the picture and enlarged it on her screen. The girl looked to be about the right age, and her eyes—they stared directly at Maggie through the computer—her eyes were unmistakable. Brown. Bright. Maggie's. The girl had Maggie's eyes. Maggie blinked trying to clear her vision suddenly obscured by tears. She examined the rest of the young woman's face. She could easily pass for Maggie's daughter.

How was this possible? Was it possible? Things like this only happened in the movies, not in real life. And this was about as real as it gets. Maggie clicked once again on the *Information* tab. West Hill High School. *Relatives*, mother—was she her real mother, or was that an honor denied to Maggie—Hannah Kennedy.

Maggie clicked on Hannah's name. She scrolled through her page. There wasn't much to see, but one picture caught Maggie's attention. It was a picture of Cassidy in a cap and gown. She must have just graduated from high school, putting her in the right age range. Hannah Kennedy's profile photo was a picture of a florist shop. Her job was listed as self-employed, owner of Petals of Love. A quick Google search gave Maggie the address, only twenty minutes away.

❖

"Bad idea," Maggie said out loud. Bad idea. Bad idea. Her brain screamed. She pulled into the parking lot next to the building and sat in the car for a full ten minutes trying to talk herself into going in. Or maybe she was trying to talk herself into *not* going in. She wasn't sure. Thinking straight didn't seem to be in her wheelhouse in that moment. She took a deep breath, got out of her car, straightened the hem of her shirt, and walked into Petals of Love.

She had managed to find one picture of Hannah on her Facebook page. It was blurry, taken from some distance away. There weren't many pictures and what was there were mostly of Cassidy or flowers.

The twenty-minute drive gave Maggie plenty of time to think about what to say once she was face-to-face with Hannah. She had come up with exactly nothing. How do you ask someone if *their* child was really *your* child? It all felt so surreal. Surely there was a mix-up with the DNA samples. That was easy enough to believe. What wasn't so easy to dismiss was how much Cassidy Kennedy resembled Maggie.

Maggie jumped at the sound of a bell overhead as she pushed the door open. There was only one person in the shop, a woman behind the counter. She looked up from whatever she was doing, and a smile spread across her face. It seemed genuine, not one of those forced smiles you often see on salespeople.

"Hi there. Welcome to Petals of Love. Feel free to look around. I'll be with you in just a moment." Even from this distance Maggie could tell she had bright blue eyes. The woman gave her attention once more to the pile of papers in front of her. It gave Maggie a few moments to study her. She was pretty, dark blond hair, light complexion, medium build. About five foot four, Maggie guessed. She looked nothing like the pictures of Cassidy that Maggie saw on Facebook. More proof that Cassidy might be hers and not Hannah's.

The shop was small, but boasted a large array of flowers, from simple bouquets by the counter and roses in the cooler to every sort of paraphernalia for houseplants and even fairy gardens.

This was crazy. Maggie's heart was beating so hard that it was making her feel light-headed. This *was* a bad idea. What had she been thinking? Even if there had been an embryo switch this wasn't the way to handle it. She turned and headed toward the door.

"Is this your first time here?" Hannah was right behind her. She turned to the sound of her voice.

Hannah had never seen the woman before, yet there was something so familiar about her. "Do we know each other?" she asked. Sometimes it was hard to place a person when you saw them out of the setting you were used to seeing them in.

"Um, no. I don't believe so. I've...I've never...I mean I haven't been in your shop before."

The woman had stunning dark brown eyes, her long hair almost as dark. There was an outdoors ruggedness about her. A well-tanned freshness, a natural beauty. Hannah caught herself staring. It had been a long time since she was drawn to a woman, and she couldn't remember a time she was so drawn to a total stranger. The visceral response in her body was startling. A quick glance at the woman's left hand showed no wedding ring. Hannah had a feeling that they played for the same team. Her gaydar was seldom wrong. "We haven't met somewhere else, by chance? Maybe at a school event?"

"I don't have any children so that isn't possible."

Hannah had the urge to ask her out. She mentally kicked herself. She wasn't the kind to do such things. What would this woman think of her being so forward? She purposely redirected her train of thought. "What can I do for you? Were you looking for something specific?"

"What?" A look of confusion crossed her face.

"Flowers? Were you looking for something specific? For a sweetheart maybe?" *Smooth. She is a customer. Stop fishing for personal information.*

"Umm, flowers. Right. No. No sweetheart. Um..." She looked around.

She seemed to be stumbling over her words. Was it possible she was feeling the same instant attraction?

"I came in for..." Her eyes were intense and seemed to look directly into Hannah.

So much so that Hannah felt suddenly exposed. It confused her.

"Um. For daisies. Do you have any daisies?" She broke the eye contact and looked around the shop.

Daisies? That was a little unusual. "Are you looking for an arrangement or a bouquet?"

"Bouquet, I guess."

"I can certainly put that together for you. Would you like other flowers as well?" Hannah suggested a few other flowers that would complement the white daisies.

"Yeah. Okay. That would be good." Her eyes darted about, looking everywhere but at Hannah now.

"Which ones?"

"Any of them. Whatever you think would look good."

Hannah stared at her longer than she knew she should. She couldn't quite figure her out. "Okay. That will just take a few minutes."

No response.

"Does that work for you? Miss…?"

Again, no response. Saying *miss* like that usually got someone to say their name. This woman, however, did not.

The woman suddenly turned to her and gave Hannah a smile that lit up her whole face, making her even more attractive. "Yes. That's fine. Thank you."

Even her strange behavior couldn't squash the attraction Hannah was feeling for her. It was all very weird. She must be having a rough day Hannah surmised. If that was the case, Hannah wished she could make it better for her. She set about putting a bouquet together, filled with mostly daisies, all the while wondering how she could get this woman's phone number.

What the hell? She didn't ask strange women for their phone numbers. She didn't drool over women she hardly knew—didn't really know at all. Not that she was actually drooling. That would have been gross and very unprofessional.

She took her time with the flowers, sneaking glances while the woman wandered around the shop. *Nice ass. Stop it!*

The bell over the door rang again, announcing another customer. Mr. Thomas waltzed in like he owned the place. The elderly gentleman had bought so many flowers for his wife that he might as well have taken out stock in the place. "It's Bernice's birthday tomorrow, so we need to do something extra special for her," he announced.

"Of course," Hannah answered. "I'll be right with you."

He nodded.

Hannah finished the bouquet she was working on and wrapped a red ribbon around it. "All set. What do you think?" She held the flowers up.

"Beautiful." The smile was gone again. The woman handed Hannah two twenty-dollar bills.

Hannah was disappointed that she didn't pay by credit card or check so Hannah would at least have her name. "Let me get you your change."

"That's okay. Keep it. As a tip." She took the flowers and was gone. The sound of the bell over the door seemed to echo through the shop much longer than it usually did.

Hannah just stared after her. How strange was that?

"I need something with lots of red roses," Mr. Thomas said.

Hannah pushed thoughts of the attractive woman away. Time to get back to business as usual.

❖

Maggie threw the bouquet of flowers in the back seat with so much force the plastic wrap split open and the flowers scattered across the seat and floor.

"What the hell was I thinking. I shouldn't have done that. I shouldn't have gone in there." She let out a loud groan. That woman—Hannah Kennedy—must have thought she was crazy. She could barely speak to her. She sure as hell couldn't find the words to ask her about the possibility of Cassidy being *her* daughter, not Hannah's. When it hit her that one of her embryos had survived, she couldn't contain that stupid smile. She must have seemed like a mad woman.

She was convinced that Cassidy was her child. She felt it in her very soul. Maybe the emptiness she had felt for so long wasn't because she didn't have a child. Maybe it was because she *did* have a child, but never held her in her arms.

It was all so confusing. The laughing fit that overtook her bordered on hysterical and morphed into sobs. She managed to drive a couple of blocks and pull over. The last thing she needed was for Hannah to come out and see her in this condition.

With her emotions finally somewhat under control, she drove to her sister's house. She was relieved to find only her sister's Toyota in the driveway. Darrel, Jean's husband, was probably still at work.

The sobs that had racked her earlier returned as soon as Jean answered the door.

"Oh my God, Maggie. What's wrong?"

"I have a daughter," Maggie managed to squeak out.

"What are you talking about? Come in here." Maggie followed her into the kitchen. It was the biggest room in the house, by design. Jean's favorite thing to do was cook and she owned every kitchen gadget ever invented. A spotless set of stainless-steel pots and pans hung from a wrought iron rack over a granite covered island. An oak table sat against one wall, just large enough for Jean's family of four. Any more than that and the large table in the dining room was employed.

Jean poured her a glass of water from the pitcher in the fridge. "Sit. Tell me what's going on."

Maggie sat at the island and took the glass Jean handed her. Jean leaned on the counter across from her. She had the same brown eyes that Maggie had inherited from their father. The same brown eyes that Cassidy had in her Facebook picture.

Maggie sipped the water as she tried to formulate the right words to explain.

Jean ran a hand through her short salt-and-pepper hair and then tapped her fingers on the counter. Patience had never been her strong suit. "Maggie?"

"Do you remember when I turned thirty and I wasn't in a relationship but wanted a baby more than anything?"

"Of course. I remember how devastated you were when you had trouble conceiving and then when the in vitro failed."

Maggie nodded. "I have a daughter."

"Are you adopting?"

"No. I mean I have a biological daughter."

"Maggie, I was there with you when you took the pregnancy test. It was negative. The whole ordeal wiped you out emotionally and financially. You said you couldn't go through it again." Jean stopped and seemed to think. "You didn't try again, did you? You couldn't have." She paused. "I'm confused."

"I didn't try again. There must have been a mix-up with the embryos. One of mine was implanted in someone else and she gave birth to my daughter."

"Wait. How could that have happened? How do you know? Who is the person that got your embryo? Are you sure? There's a baby out there that's yours?"

"That's how I feel. I have so many questions. She's not a baby." Maggie told Jean about the email, checking the ancestry site, and everything she had done up until this point.

"So, you saw the woman who gave birth to her—Cassidy—but you didn't tell her who you are?

Maggie nodded. "I fully intended to talk to her about it but just couldn't find the words. I acted like a jerk. She must have thought I was just an insane customer."

"What are you going to do now? I assume you want to meet Cassidy. You know you have grounds for a lawsuit."

"Of course, I want to meet her. I want to *know* her and have her know me. I'm not sure how to proceed."

"Maybe you should hire a lawyer to make contact."

"Why?"

"I don't know. That's how they would do it in the movies. And you'll need a lawyer if you're going to sue that damn fertility clinic."

"It is way too soon to even think about that. I missed out on years of my daughter's life. I don't want to miss out on any more. I have to figure out a way to contact her without upsetting her."

"Do you think she knows? That her mother—birth mother—non-biological mother isn't her real mother?"

"I'm pretty sure she would have gotten an email with her results. I don't think they would have notified me unless she gave them permission to add relatives to her family tree and it would list me as her mother. So, she must know something."

"But they haven't tried to contact you? Maybe they are in denial."

"I would imagine they are in just as much shock as I am. It can't be easy."

Jean went into her pantry and returned with a bottle of honey whiskey. "I think we need something stronger than water." She poured a generous amount into two glasses and added ice. "Do you have a way to contact this girl without going back to her mother—it doesn't seem right to call her that—sorry. Anyway, can you contact her?"

"I can message her through the Genetic Experts site. Do you think I should do that?"

"Yeah. I think you should," Jean said.

Maggie took a large swig of her drink. It burned her throat and she let out an *ugh* and shuddered. She wasn't used to hard liquor. Beer was much more her thing.

Jean disappeared down the hall and returned with her laptop. "Do it now while you have the courage."

"Who said I have courage?"

"Then do it now while you have the nerve."

Nerve? Did she have the nerve? Did she have the right? Yes. Not only did she have the right to know her daughter, but her daughter had the right to get to know her. And to know the truth. It wasn't Maggie's fault that somebody had fucked up and her embryo had been implanted in someone else. She wasn't about to apologize for it or for wanting to make it right. Maybe Jean was correct. Do it now. Get the truth out there and let the chips fall where they may. She could do it delicately, try not to ruffle too many feathers. Try not to upset the apple cart. Try not to do any number of other clichés.

She pulled up the site, typed her password in, and clicked on Cassidy's name. She stared at the empty message box for several minutes before typing.

Dear Miss Kennedy…backspace…erase…start again.

Dear Cassidy,

As you probably noticed, I'm your mother…*backspace*… *erase*…*start again.*

As you probably noticed in your DNA results, I am listed as your mother. This is probably a terrible shock. But it's true... backspace...erase...start again.

It took Maggie a full twenty minutes to come up with an acceptable message.

Dear Cassidy,

As you probably noticed in your DNA results, I am listed as your mother. You may be confused by this. I was as well. After giving it a lot of thought I have concluded that there may have been a mix-up at the fertility place, North Hampton Clinic, that I (and I assume your mother) used almost nineteen years ago. I believe that you may indeed be my biological daughter. I'm not trying to upset you or intrude on your life. I would, however, love the opportunity to get to know you, as well as the mother who raised you. I would really appreciate hearing from you. You can message me back on this site or better yet you can text or call. I look forward to your response.

Maggie Walsh

She included her address and phone number and hit *send* before she had a chance to change her mind.

CHAPTER FIVE

"Mom, I don't understand this." Cassidy was visibly upset. "Why would this woman think she's my mother? This is a mistake. Right?" Cassidy pulled her feet off the coffee table and sat upright. How many times had Hannah told her to keep her feet on the floor?

Hannah sat beside her. She wished she could reassure Cassidy that, yes indeed, this was a mistake. But her heart told her that it probably wasn't. Maggie Walsh had used the same clinic that she and Teri had used, and it seemed that it was about the same time frame too. She mentally kicked herself for not following through with the private detective idea and checking this out herself first.

"Mom?"

There was no way around this. She had to be honest. "Honey, I think there's a chance that it's not a mistake."

"No way. There is no way you aren't my *real* mom."

Hannah pulled her daughter—how much longer could she use that term—into her arms. "Oh, honey, no matter what happens, I *am* your real mom. Nothing could change that." She pulled back far enough to look into Cassidy's eyes. "You *know* that right? Nothing can ever change the relationship between us. You are my kiddo, no matter what."

"I don't understand this."

"Me either. But we can get to the bottom of it. If this woman is your…" Hannah let the words trail off. She couldn't say it. She could barely even think it. "I guess we need to find out for sure. Maybe it is all a mistake. But we need to find out. For your sake as well as for her sake."

"I don't want to. I don't want to know anything about her or about this."

"I know, honey, but we can't just ignore it. I wish we could. But I think it's only right to respond and get to the truth." Hannah decided not to mention the possibility that Maggie had been implanted with her embryo and there might be another child out there. A child that was biologically Hannah's.

"I don't want to," Cassidy repeated. "Can you do it?"

"You want me to contact her?"

"I don't want anyone to, but if you say we *have* to, then yes. I want you to do it."

"All right. I can do that. We'll see what she has to say. But we need to prepare ourselves in case it turns out that she's right." How they were supposed to do that, Hannah had no idea. Her gut told her that the truth was staring them in the face. A truth that there was no getting around.

"Do you want to use my phone to message her back?"

Hannah thought about it for a few moments. "No, just forward me the message so I have her number. I'll call her if I can work up the nerve and text her if I can't." She gave Cassidy another hug. "It will all be okay. I promise." She hoped it was a promise she could keep.

❖

It took Hannah another day and a half before she could talk herself into texting Maggie Walsh. Her message was simple.

Hello. My daughter, Cassidy, got your message and asked me to reply. I do believe there could have been a mix-up with the embryos. I would like to discuss this further with you so we can be sure.—Hannah

A response came almost immediately.

Thank you so much for your text. I know this must be upsetting for you and Cassidy, as it is for me. I would be happy to answer any questions you may have. I hope you feel the same. I am open to ideas on how to proceed.

Hannah was surprised and not prepared when the text arrived so quickly. Without letting herself think about it, for fear of backing out, she typed out her response.

Can we meet? Let me know a time and location that works for you and I'll arrange my schedule. Thanks in advance.

She hit *send* and immediately felt sick to her stomach. Cassidy was eighteen. There would be no custody fight, but she was sure Maggie Walsh would want Cassidy in her life. Would that be good or detrimental to Cassidy? Could she lose a part of Cassidy to this other woman? She'd had her daughter all to herself for the past sixteen years. It wasn't that she wasn't willing to share her. Or was it? She didn't know. So many emotions swirled through her, wreaking havoc on her body.

She stared at her phone, expecting an immediate response. It took quite a while for one to come through. She was waiting on a couple of customers when she heard her phone ping behind the counter. It was all she could do to keep her attention on the task at hand and the young woman and her mother she was helping decide on flower arrangements for a wedding. The bride was so picky and her mother was trying to get her to ease up on her demands. It was another half an hour before the mother handed Hannah her credit card for the deposit. She grabbed her phone as soon as they were out the door.

How about tomorrow at the Fairway Café? Does two o'clock work for you?

Tomorrow? That was so soon. And the Fairway Café was only a few blocks away. This Maggie Walsh must live in the area or close by. Hannah hadn't even thought about the possibility that she could be in the same town. They could have passed each other numerous times on the street or in the grocery store. The stranger who could be her daughter's biological mother—not could be—*was*—her daughter's biological mother, could be anyone and Hannah would have never known.

❖

Shit. Maggie hadn't considered that it might be Hannah who requested to see her. But of course, that made sense. She would want to check Maggie out before letting her anywhere near Cassidy. Maggie would probably have done the same.

Would Hannah recognize her from the other day in the flower shop, when Maggie had made a fool of herself? More than likely yes. But Hannah must see tons of people in her shop, she reasoned. *Maybe she won't remember me.*

But Maggie knew the chances of that were slim. Oh, why didn't she tell Hannah who she was and why she was there? Better yet, why did she go in the first place? There was no getting around it now. She would just explain and hope that Hannah understood.

She'd googled restaurants near Hannah's shop to make it as convenient for Hannah as possible. She could make it very difficult for Maggie to have any kind of a relationship with Cassidy if she wanted to. Not smart to make an enemy of her right from the start.

She was starting to worry when she didn't hear back from Hannah for a full thirty-five minutes. Her response was straight to the point.

See you there.

Okay. It was on. This was real now. She called Jean to give her a quick update.

"How are you feeling?" Jean asked her.

"Nervous. I feel like this is a dream or an LSD trip or something. Or at least what I think an LSD trip would feel like. It just doesn't seem real. One email and my whole world has been turned upside down."

"I can only imagine. I'm sorry you have to go through this. Do you want me to go with you? I can take off from work."

"I appreciate that, but this is something I need to do on my own."

"I can understand that."

"You know how much I always wanted a kid and there is a kid out there in the world that is more than likely mine. I just want to get to the other side of this."

"What do you mean?"

"I want to get through all this preliminary stuff and get to know her. I hope she wants to get to know me too. This must be so confusing for her."

They talked for another twenty minutes, with Jean doing most of the listening and throwing in a question or suggestion here and there. Maggie felt drained and emotionally exhausted by the time they hung up.

She made her evening rounds in the barns to make sure all the horses were set for the night, even though it was Randi's job. Maggie always slept better when she saw for herself that everything was done. Not that she didn't trust Randi, because she did. Maggie just liked to see for herself.

Satisfied that all was well, she settled down in front of the TV with a beer. The screen flashed in front of her without her taking any of it in. Her mind went again and again to what she should say when she met with Hannah the following day. The reel continued to play when she laid her head down in bed. She barely got any sleep at all. How could she when she would be meeting the mother of her daughter in less than twenty-four hours?

❖

Hannah was wired and tired as she sat at one of the tables outside at the Fairway Café a full thirty minutes early. Sleep had eluded her the night before. She hadn't told Cassidy about the meeting with Maggie yet. She didn't want her stewing about it. She would fill her in later. Her stomach felt like it had been turned inside out.

"Can I get you anything to drink?"

She hadn't noticed the waitress approaching and she jumped. *Calm your ass down. You can do this.* "Can I get a cup of coffee, please? I'm waiting for someone to join me."

"Very good." She disappeared as quietly as she had arrived.

Hannah pulled her phone from her back pocket and sent a text to Becca, her employee.

Hannah: *How's it going?*

Becca: *You just left ten minutes ago. It's going fine. Are you okay?*

Hannah: *Yes. Why are you asking me that?*

Becca: *Because you seemed like you were ready to crawl out of your skin when you left here.*

Hannah: *I'm fine. Just a lot on my mind. Text me if you have any problems.*

Becca: *Stop worrying. I've got this covered.*

Hannah: *Ok. Ok. Thanks.*

Hannah looked up from her phone just in time to see the same woman who had purchased the daisy bouquet a few days earlier. She looked even more attractive with the sunlight bouncing off her brown hair and tanned skin. Her tight jeans hugged her body in ways Hannah wished she could. Her button-down shirt had short sleeves that revealed well-toned arms. Hannah had the urge to stop her, chat her up, and possibly ask for her phone number. These thoughts and urges were so unlike her. But now was not the time. Not when she was expecting Maggie Walsh. The last thing she needed was for Maggie to show up while she was flirting with some woman, no matter how attractive Hannah found that woman to be.

She tried not to stare as the woman got closer and wondered if she was going to walk by or stop for a late lunch at the café. She was shocked when the woman walked right up to her.

"Hannah." It was more of a statement than a question.

Hannah was confused. How did she know her name?

"Yes."

"I'm Maggie." She put out her hand.

Hannah just stared at it. This was Maggie? Cassidy's Maggie? What? "You're Maggie? But…" She let the word linger in the air. "No sense asking for your phone number, seeing I already have it," Hannah muttered sarcastically.

"What?"

"Nothing. How long have you known who I am? I'm sure you knew when you came into my floral shop. What exactly did you think you were doing?" Her confusion was quickly replaced by anger.

"May I sit down and explain?"

Hannah waved a hand toward the empty chair across from her.

Maggie sat but didn't say anything.

"Well?" Hannah said.

Maggie visibly swallowed. Hard. "Yes, I knew who you were. I did some research soon after getting the notification that Cassidy was my daughter."

"We don't know that for sure, yet. There is still the possibility of an error with the DNA." She wasn't sure if she was trying to convince Maggie or herself. Looking closely at the woman sitting across from her she could see the resemblance to Cassidy. Hannah should have done some research on her own like she had intended to do. She felt like she was at a disadvantage here, with Maggie knowing about her, but Hannah knowing nothing about Maggie.

"Isn't that why I'm here? So, we can figure that out?"

"Go on. You researched, I'm assuming, Cassidy *and* me. You decided to spy on me?"

"No. That's not how it was. I went to your shop to talk to you about this and lost my nerve. I just couldn't get the words out. Even now this seems so unreal." She paused, like she was waiting for Hannah to respond.

Hannah was at a loss for words. She realized she was staring.

"I brought these," Maggie said as she slipped several photos from a large envelope that Hannah had failed to notice.

"What's this?"

"I saw a few pictures of Cassidy online. These are pictures of me around the same age. I'm guessing that Cassidy is about seventeen or eighteen." She slid the pictures across the table to Hannah.

"She's eighteen." Hannah kept her eyes on Maggie for several long moments, afraid to look down. Afraid to see the truth that the photos likely held. She slowly brought her eyes down and picked up the picture from the top of the pile. There it was. The young woman in the photo looked so much like Cassidy that she could have passed as her sister—or her mother. She let out a long, trembling breath. There was no need to see the rest. Her eyes filled with tears.

The hand Maggie laid on top of hers was momentarily comforting. "I can only imagine how hard this is for you."

Hannah pulled her hand away. "You don't know what I'm going through."

"You're right. I don't. But you don't know what it's like to have a child in the world that you didn't get to give birth to or raise. That's the pain that has ripped into *my* heart." She tapped her chest.

Did that answer the question Hannah had yet to ask? "You didn't have a baby? You went to the same fertility clinic we used."

Maggie closed her eyes and shook her head. When she opened her eyes again, she looked directly at Hannah. "They implanted two embryos. Neither one survived."

Two. They implanted two in Hannah as well. One developed. One did not. Hannah wondered if both had been Maggie's. Either way, both of her embryos had died. That was over eighteen years ago, but the news was as fresh as the tears that rolled down her cheeks.

Hannah was the lucky one. The one who got to raise Cassidy. Maggie didn't expect her to look so sad. She stifled the urge to comfort her.

"What exactly is it that you want?"

What did she want? She wanted to go back eighteen years and have the opportunity to raise a daughter. *Her* daughter. But that was impossible. "I want to get to know Cassidy. I have no intention of taking her away from you."

"What if she doesn't want to get to know you?"

Had Maggie even considered that possibility? No. She hadn't. She had had such a desire to know her own mother, who had abandoned them, that she thought for sure Cassidy would want to know her once she knew the truth. "Did she say that?" She braced herself for an answer she didn't want to hear.

"She didn't want to contact you at all. She doesn't want her world turned upside down."

"I don't plan—"

The waitress chose that moment to interrupt them. "Would you like something to drink?" she asked Maggie. "Or are you ready to order?"

The last thing Maggie wanted right now was food. "Can I just get a glass of water?"

"Sure thing. Need a refill on that coffee?"

Maggie peered over at Hannah's full cup.

Hannah shook her head. "I think we're all set for right now. Thank you."

Maggie waited until the waitress was out of earshot before she continued. "I don't want to do anything to upset Cassidy or make her life harder. But I've missed out on years of her life. I don't intend on missing any more of it."

"And just what *do* you intend to do?"

Maggie hadn't known what to expect, but this wasn't it. She softened the tone of her voice. "I'm hoping as a mother, you can see my point of view. I think if we give Cassidy some time to get used to the idea, she will come around."

"What about Cassidy's biological father? Is he going to want to be in her life as well?"

"There is no father."

"Immaculate conception? Should we call the Bible people and tell them to update it?"

Maggie couldn't help but laugh. She could see Hannah trying to suppress a smile, but the corners of her mouth turned up anyway. She was much prettier when she smiled. She wasn't sure how much she should share with Hannah. On the off chance that she was homophobic, it might be better to leave out the fact that she was gay. "I used artificial insemination. I was single, just turned thirty, and wanted a baby so badly that I did it all on my own."

She could see Hannah's face soften. "And you didn't get one. I'm sorry." She sounded sincere. "How come you didn't try again?"

"The first round of IVF nearly bankrupted me. As you must know, it isn't cheap. I couldn't afford to try again. I had just started my business, a horse stable, and money was tight. It takes time for something like that to turn a profit. By the time it did, the doctors told me I wasn't able to carry a child. A problem with my uterus."

"Why didn't you adopt?"

Because agencies weren't keen on handing newborns to a single lesbian at that time, she thought but didn't say out loud. "It just wasn't in the cards, I guess." The waitress returned with her glass of water and she took a large swig. "What about you? Do you and your husband have other children?"

"No." Hannah seemed to hesitate. "My wife died when Cassidy was two. I raised her on my own."

Wife? Probably not a homophobe then. Maggie nearly laughed out loud. "Wife, huh?"

"Yes. My wife. We brought a baby into a very loving home." She sounded defensive.

"Same-sex marriage wasn't legal in all fifty states until two thousand fifteen. Of course, Massachusetts legalized it in two thousand four."

Hannah looked surprised that Maggie knew that. "We had a commitment ceremony two years before Cassidy was born and got married in Massachusetts as soon as it was legal there. Not that any of that matters to you." Defensive again.

Maggie put up her hands. "I'm not judging. That would be a little hypocritical of me. Don't you think? I mean, considering I'm gay."

Hannah tilted her head and stared at her. Trying to decide if she was telling the truth, Maggie figured. The brief silence gave Maggie a chance to take Hannah in. To really see her. She looked a little different in the sunlight than she did under the harsh fluorescent lights. Her dark blond hair seemed a little lighter and her blue eyes a little brighter. Full lips with just the slightest touch of makeup. Pretty. Very pretty.

Maggie wondered if Hannah ever thought about the fact that Cassidy didn't look like her. At. All.

"Walsh is an Irish name isn't it?" Hannah said at last. Obviously changing the subject.

"Yes."

"Cassidy's DNA results showed no Irish at all. Can you explain that?"

Hannah seemed to be grasping at straws. Didn't the pictures convince her that Cassidy was Maggie's child? Hell, didn't the damn DNA? "My grandfather was adopted by an Irish couple when he was a toddler. His parents, both Italian, died in a car accident. His adoptive parents gave him their last name."

Hannah nodded, apparently satisfied with the answer.

"The picture I found of Cassidy on Facebook—yes, I Facebook stalked her—showed her standing next to a horse. Does she ride?"

Hannah thought for a moment. Maggie owned a horse stable. Cassidy had loved horses since she was little. Obviously, some things were nature as opposed to nurture. "She does. She rides and gives lessons as well."

"I've been riding forever and even competed when I was younger. I gave up the stress of competing to focus on more casual forms of riding and teaching. Maybe you could bring Cassidy to the stables. She might be more comfortable meeting me if she's around horses."

This was all happening too fast. It was less than a week ago that Hannah found out about Maggie. It was a lot for her brain to compute. But Maggie did have a point. Cassidy would probably be much more open to the idea of meeting Maggie if it was at the stables. A part of her hoped that Cassidy would all-out refuse to meet her. But another part—the mother part—knew that would be very unfair to Maggie. It wasn't Maggie's fault that someone else had given birth to and raised her child.

"I'll talk to her about it," Hannah said.

"That's all I ask." Maggie smiled. "Can I buy you lunch as long as we're here?"

The woman Hannah had been so attracted to a few days ago was offering to buy her lunch. She would have jumped at the chance if circumstances were different. Her gaydar had been correct after all. But this was the woman who was going to disrupt their lives, granted, through no fault of her own, but disrupt them nonetheless. "I have to get back to the shop."

The smile faded, and for a moment, Hannah wanted to bring it back. "Of course. Another time then."

Hannah rose, her coffee untouched. She put a five-dollar bill on the table.

"Please keep in touch," Maggie said. "Please."

Hannah nodded. She walked back to the shop without looking back. Her head was swirling. No wonder she had thought she knew Maggie from somewhere when she had walked into her shop. Cassidy had her eyes, and their faces had a very similar shape. She couldn't believe she had been so attracted to her. That wasn't true. She could believe it. But that was then. This was now. And now everything had changed. Hannah wasn't sure how she was going to deal with that change.

Chapter Six

I met with Maggie." Hannah put the bowl of salad in the middle of the table.

Cassidy's eyes got wide. "You did? Why didn't you tell me?"

"I'm telling you now." Hannah sat across from her. She put a scoop of mashed potatoes on her plate and passed the bowl to Cassidy.

"So?" Cassidy raised her eyebrows.

"She seems nice."

"You know that's not what I'm asking."

Yeah. Hannah knew. Cassidy wasn't going to like the truth. "I'm convinced that she is your biological mother. I know that's not what you wanted. But there's no way around it."

Cassidy pushed her plate forward. "How can you be sure?"

"She had pictures of herself at your age. The resemblance was unmistakable. You look like her, especially your eyes."

"I don't care. You're my mother. She's nothing to me."

That was the response Hannah was hoping for in her heart. She wouldn't force Cassidy to see her, but she needed to at least present Maggie's case. It was only fair. Not that anything about this whole situation was fair. "Yes. I'm your mother. Nothing will ever change that. Maggie owns a horse stable, I guess she gives lessons and stuff. She loves horses. Just like you do."

Hannah watched the expression on Cassidy's face change. Soften. If there was anything she loved in this world as much as she loved Hannah, it was horses. There were times Hannah was convinced that she came in second to her love of them.

"Maggie suggested that you go to the stable to meet her. She just wants the chance to get to know you." Hannah put her fork down and folded her hands. "I think you should consider it, honey. If I were in her position, I would want to meet you. I can't image having a child out there that I don't know." She gave Cassidy a few minutes to absorb the information. "What do you think?"

"What stable is it?" The question was not surprising.

"I didn't ask."

"Where is it?"

"I didn't ask." *Guess I failed to get the most important information.* Hannah almost laughed out loud at the irony. "I can find out, if that makes a difference."

"It doesn't make a difference. I was just curious."

Hannah wasn't so sure Cassidy was telling the whole truth. Maggie having a horse stable did seem to make a difference to her.

"I'll find out. Do you think it would be okay if I set up a time for you to go?" Hannah asked.

Cassidy shrugged.

It wasn't exactly a no. "I'll text Maggie and see if she's got time on Monday. You still have Monday off, don't you?" She waited to see if Cassidy would object. She didn't. Her nod was barely noticeable, but she did nod.

So, there it was. She was going to set up a meeting between her daughter and Maggie. She didn't know how to feel. Or maybe she did, and she was just too afraid to feel it.

"Mom, make sure Becca is covering the shop. I'm not going there without you."

She wasn't planning on letting Cassidy go by herself. She felt the need to support her daughter through this. "Okay." Becca was scheduled for Monday anyway, and Mondays weren't that busy. She should be able to handle it without Hannah.

Hannah hoped she and Cassidy could handle the day at Maggie Walsh's.

❖

"You're either going to give yourself carpal tunnel or wear a hole in that poor horse," Randi said to Maggie.

She'd been brushing Clover for the last—she didn't know how long. Spending time with the horses helped calm her nerves. Usually. Today there was no settling them down. Cassidy and Hannah were on their way. Excitement. Fear. Self-doubt. So many things were swirling through her.

She handed the brush to Randi. "Can you get Clover, Milkshake, and Jake ready for a ride? I'm hoping Cassidy and her mother..." She paused. She was Cassidy's mother. But she wasn't her mom and she never would be. She needed to remember that. It hurt her heart and made her head spin. "Anyway, I'm hoping they'll agree to go for a ride. If Cassidy is anything like me, she'll find it's easier to relax if her ass is in a saddle."

Randi laughed. "Language, boss. You don't want to be talking like that around Cassidy."

"She's a teenager. I'm sure she's heard that word before. Probably even said it a time or two."

Randi had been very supportive since Maggie explained the situation to her. She even brought over a fruit salad to add to the spread that Maggie put together to feed Hannah and Cassidy.

Maggie wasn't surprised when Hannah said she would be accompanying Cassidy on the visit. Maggie would have done the same thing if the situation was reversed. She was just heading back to the house when she saw their car pull into the drive. Her nerves stood at attention as she watched Cassidy exit the vehicle.

She was taller than Maggie thought she would be. Almost as tall as Maggie herself and several inches taller than Hannah. She looked so much like a younger version of herself that Maggie nearly gasped. She was dressed in what Maggie guessed was typical teenage garb, light blue jeans and a T-shirt with some faded logo on it.

Maggie put her hand out when she reached them. She thought a hug, which was really what she wanted to do, might seem too forward. She didn't want to scare Cassidy away right from the start. "Hi. You must be Cassidy. I'm Maggie. I'm so glad to meet you."

Cassidy shook the hand that was offered to her. "Um. Hi."

Maggie looked over at Hannah and mouthed the words *thank you*. "Good to see you again, Hannah," she said. "Come on in. I've got lunch ready. I hope you're hungry." Even as she said the words she wondered if she would be able to get food down with the way her stomach felt. She was sure the acid must be eating its way through her.

They silently followed her into the house. It was a modest single-story ranch, but Maggie made sure it was always clean and orderly. She preferred to put her money into the stables. She spent most of her time there anyways. "Make yourselves at home. Sit anywhere. What would you like to drink? Cassidy?"

"Whiskey. Straight up," Cassidy said with a straight face as she slid onto the nearest kitchen chair.

Maggie looked from her to Hannah.

"She's joking. She said she could use a stiff drink on our way over here. She doesn't drink. At least she better not. This…" She waved her arm between them. "Is—well—strange. It's stressful for her. I'm sorry."

Maggie nodded. She understood. "No. You're right. This is a strange situation. One I'm sure you never expected to find yourselves in. I certainly didn't. But I think we can get through it. And maybe even all become friends." She turned her attention once again to Cassidy. "How about a glass of soda? I have Pepsi, Sprite, and root beer. Or iced tea."

"Water would be fine. Thank you."

Another thing in common. Maggie had only purchased the soda to give them choices. She rarely drank it herself. "Sure. For you, Hannah?"

"A glass of iced tea would be good."

"Please, Hannah, sit. Make yourself comfortable."

Hannah did as she was told.

Maggie busied herself getting the drinks and putting food on the table. She was glad to have something to do with her hands, so she wasn't wringing them together. Once everything was set, she sat. "Please. Help yourselves."

Hannah put some fruit salad and a roll on her plate. Cassidy did the same, minus the roll. Maggie filled her plate, not sure why. She really had no appetite. Apparently, neither did Cassidy or Hannah. They just picked at their food.

"Cassidy, Hannah—your mom—tells me you're into horses. You ride?"

Cassidy's eyes lit up. "Yes. I started taking lessons when I was little. I love horses."

"I thought maybe after lunch we could go for a ride, if you're interested."

"I would like that."

Maggie couldn't help but smile. The thing she loved most, horses, could be the one thing that would help her get to know her daughter. "Do you usually ride English or Western?"

"I learned both but like Western best. I give lessons to the younger kids too. Do you teach advanced dressage?"

"I do."

"I've only learned the basics. The stable I ride and teach at doesn't teach advanced."

Hannah was feeling left out. She had no idea what they were talking about and found herself watching their lips move without really hearing what they were saying. It was just short of an out-of-body experience. She was sitting next to her daughter, the daughter she gave birth to, with her daughter's biological mother sitting across from them. How many times in the universe did something like this happen? Not many, she ventured to guess. Of course, how many times was there an embryo mix-up? They should probably talk to someone at the fertility clinic and try to get answers as to how such a thing could happen.

She was yanked out of her thoughts when she realized Cassidy was talking about her. "What?"

"*What* what?" Cassidy said.

"I missed what you just said about me."

"Maggie said she had three horses saddled up and ready for us to ride. I told her you're afraid of horses."

"That's not true," Hannah said.

"So, you'll go horseback riding with us?" Maggie asked her. Oh shit. No. "Um. I would rather not."

"How come?"

"Because I'm afraid of horses." She scrunched up her face.

"That's what I said." Cassidy shook her head.

Maggie looked at her and blinked. "How could anyone be afraid of horses? They are the sweetest creatures on earth. With Cassidy riding and teaching at a stable you must be around them."

"I tend to keep my distance."

"You don't go to the stable with her? You must have brought her there when she was younger."

"I did. I go now to family day. I just don't go near the horses."

"You have sparked my curiosity. What is it about them that frightens you?"

"They are just so big and large. And big. Did I mention large?"

"You did."

"Mom, you should come riding with us. We can go slow. I would love that."

Hannah would have loved to be a part of what she seemed to share with Maggie, but she just couldn't do it. Cassidy had asked her a few times when she was younger but dropped it after Hannah turned her down for the third or fourth time. Now she was asking in front of Maggie. Hannah felt like this raised the stakes. But that fact did nothing to ease her fear. She struggled for a way to get out of it without letting Cassidy down. She didn't see a way to do that. "How about you two go today and I'll hang out by the barn?"

"I can help you," Maggie said. "It's not hard. I'll make sure you have the gentlest horse."

Hannah still wasn't convinced. "I appreciate the offer. I'm afraid I'm going to have to pass, because…" She drew the word out. "I'm afraid. I admit it. Someday, I'll work on that. But today is not the day."

"Okay. I won't push. Just let me know if you ever want private lessons. We can start with just getting used to being around a horse and slowly moving up until you're ready to ride."

Yeah, like she would ever take lessons from this woman. Especially horse lessons.

"Mom, I would really like it if you could learn to be around horses and maybe even go riding with me."

Hannah was surprised. She never realized how much it would mean to Cassidy for Hannah to be able to ride and share what Cassidy loved so much. Maybe she should rethink the lesson offer—but with someone other than Maggie Walsh.

"I'll think about it, honey."

"I'm serious about the lessons," Maggie said. "Are you ready to go riding?" she asked Cassidy.

Cassidy nodded. She had hardly touched her food. Hannah wasn't surprised. None of them had really eaten much.

Down at the barn, Maggie pointed out a bench near the fenced-in enclosure. "If you want, you can just hang out here until we get back. We won't stay out for too long."

"You can take your time. I'll be fine."

Maggie disappeared with Cassidy into the barn. When she reappeared she was wearing a cowboy hat. Hannah was surprised at how hot she looked in it. She shook the thought, and the feelings it stirred in her, away.

Cassidy had on a riding helmet and gloves.

Maggie let Randi know that they would only be needing two horses. She asked her to keep Hannah company while she and Cassidy were out on the trail. Maggie and Cassidy mounted up and started out on the trail.

They were quiet for a while as they rode at a slow but steady pace. Maggie broke the silence. "Do you think we can convince your mother to take lessons so she can ride with you sometimes?"

Cassidy laughed. Maggie was caught off guard at how much it sounded like Jenna, her sister's oldest daughter.

"I always hoped she would get over her fear. I love horses so much. I could never understand why she didn't. I guess now I know."

Maggie wondered if she should enter the door Cassidy had just cracked open. "How are you feeling about all this? I know it must be confusing."

"It is. I didn't think something like this was possible. It feels like a nightmare." She paused and seemed to think about what she had just said. "No offense."

Maggie wasn't offended. She would have been surprised if Cassidy hadn't felt that way. She was hoping over time that would change. "I can understand that. Maybe you can think of me as a friend. I just want to get to know you. I feel like I missed out on your whole life. I don't want to miss out on anymore. Does that make sense?"

Cassidy took a long time to answer. Just when Maggie was sure she wasn't going to, Cassidy said, "Yes. I guess if I had a kid I didn't know about, I would want to get to know her."

"And what about a mother you didn't know about?"

Cassidy turned and looked at her. "I have a mother."

Maggie swallowed and willed her eyes not to tear up. "Of course, you do. And she seems like a great mother. I don't want to take her place. That wouldn't be fair to anyone. I just want to be a part of your life. That part can be as big or as small as you want it to be. I'll let you set the rules. Fair enough?"

Cassidy nodded.

Maggie slowed Clover down a little and let Cassidy pull ahead. The trail narrowed a bit around the next curve. This position also gave Maggie an opportunity to watch Cassidy ride. She handled the horse like an expert. Even though Maggie had nothing to do with it, other than maybe genetics, she felt proud. "We are coming to a clearing ahead," Maggie said. "You can trot, canter, or even open it up to a full gallop if you want. Jake knows the area well. He'll do what you tell him to do. Slow down when you get to the pond on the left. We'll turn around at that point and head back."

Cassidy proved to be just as good at a full gallop as she had been with Jake walking. She slowed her horse down right where she was supposed to and gently turned him around. She waited the couple of seconds it took for Maggie to catch up and they headed back to the barn.

"You can come back and ride anytime you want to," Maggie said.

"Thanks."

"Maybe we can text in the meantime? We can get to know each other a little better that way." Maggie knew that kids these days were all about texting. She figured that might seem less invasive or threatening to Cassidy.

"Yeah. Okay. We can do that. I'll give you my number when we get back."

Yes. A small victory, but Maggie would take it. All in all, she thought today had gone well. She knew she couldn't just step into Cassidy's life and expect to be welcomed with open arms. It would take time to build a relationship. Maggie was more than willing to put in the time. She hoped Cassidy would be too.

CHAPTER SEVEN

W hat did you think?" Hannah asked Cassidy on the ride home.

"She seems okay. I like that she has horses."

Hannah wondered if she should press further. She was hoping to get a better handle on what Cassidy was *feeling*. She wasn't sure she could put her own feelings into words, she probably shouldn't expect Cassidy to be able to. "Kind of funny that you love horses so much and she has a stable. Isn't it?"

"Yeah." Cassidy continued to stare out the car window.

She knew it was ridiculous, but Hannah was jealous of the fact that Maggie and Cassidy had their love of horses in common. That was something Hannah could never share with her. Or could she? If she took lessons like Maggie suggested, could she get over her fear? There were probably plenty of places she could go to. Maggie wasn't her only option. She would do an internet search when they got home. She decided not to tell Cassidy in case it didn't work out. No sense getting her hopes up.

Cassidy was quiet the rest of the ride home. She took a quick shower and headed to bed early. Hannah wasn't surprised. The day had been emotionally draining as well as confusing for them both.

Hannah poured herself a glass of wine, grabbed her laptop from the kitchen table, and settled down in the living room. She was surprised to find there were only three horse stables listed within fifty miles. One was Horizon Stables, where Cassidy rode and worked. That one was out. Another was Rocking Horse Stables, Maggie's place. The third, Green Acres, was about forty miles away. Kind of far. But not impossible. She clicked on the *Lessons* tab.

We are fully booked for the summer. Please check back in September.

Shit. Great. Just great. There went that idea. She was as relieved as she was disappointed. She closed the laptop and set it next to her on the couch. She reached for the television remote just as her phone pinged with an incoming text.

It was from Maggie. *Thank you so much for bringing Cassidy today. I really enjoyed meeting her as well as seeing you again.*

Hannah responded with a thumbs up. She set her phone down, gave it another thought, and grabbed it again. She felt like she needed to respond better than that. *Thank you for letting her ride. It helped.*

Maggie: *Of course. I know that being around horses relaxes me. I figured it would make the day easier for her.*

Hannah: *It did.*

Maggie: *I'm glad. Can I ask you a question?*

Hannah never liked it when someone asked her that. What followed was usually a question she didn't want to answer. But how did you say no, you can't ask me a question.

Hannah: *Sure*

Maggie: *Did Cassidy say anything about me or the day? I guess what I want to know is if she's handling this ok.*

Hannah: *She didn't say much of anything. She did say she liked that you have horses.*

Maggie: *I guess that's something. If you think anything I say or do is upsetting to her, will you please let me know?*

Hannah: *ok*

Hannah: *Were you serious about helping me get over my fear of horses?*

Maggie: *Of course. I think I can really help. I used to do horse therapy.*

Hannah: *Horses need therapy?*

Maggie: *LOL Let me rephrase. I used horses as therapy for troubled kids.*

Hannah: *Are you saying I'm troubled or I'm like a kid?*

Maggie: *LOL neither*

Hannah: *If you really mean it, then I would like to do this. For Cassidy.*

Maggie: *You're a good mom. Let me check my schedule and get back to you with some dates and times.*

Hannah: *thank you*

Hannah shook her head. She must be crazy. Horses scared the hell out of her. She wasn't sure why. But she did know why she wanted to try to get over it. For Cassidy. Plain and simple.

She didn't think a horse could *actually* kill her, but a heart attack might.

❖

As promised, Maggie sent several days and times that she would be available for lessons. She and Hannah settled on late afternoon on Tuesday. Cassidy would be working so she wouldn't question where Hannah was going.

Hannah arrived right on time. She pulled in the driveway and parked next to what she assumed was Maggie's car. A little farther ahead, parked in the driveway, there was a truck and horse trailer. That made sense. Hannah pictured Maggie as more of the horse riding, truck driving type.

Maggie met her in the driveway before she even had a chance to get out of the car. "Hi there. Ready to face your fears?" she asked Hannah.

"Not really, but I'm here now. I hope you have smelling salts handy in case I faint." Hannah was only half kidding. *Feel the fear and do it anyway.* She had repeated that mantra to herself over and over as she drove to the stable.

"I promise you won't faint."

"How about throwing up. Do you promise I won't do that?"

"Oh God. I hope not. That would just be gross." Maggie smiled.

Hannah laughed. Under different circumstances she could see them becoming friends, maybe even more than friends. She'd found Maggie attractive before she knew who she was or what role she would play in their lives, and she found her attractive now. Especially when she smiled.

"I normally start my lessons by having my students muck the stalls. I've got the wheelbarrow and pitchfork ready for you."

"I hope you're joking?"

"Come on. You don't like shoveling shit?"

"Doesn't everyone?"

"I'm kidding. I've got my smallest, gentlest horse in the corral. We're going to work with him. No mucking around."

Hannah followed Maggie to where the horse was tied to the fence. The corral, as Maggie had called it, was made up of three separated sections, divided by a fence. It looked as though the center part could be moved to make it into one big area. The barn was massive. It looked to be two stories high, although Hannah had no idea what you would use the second level for.

Hannah walked halfway to the horse and stopped. If this was the smallest horse, she didn't want to meet the biggest. She had to admit that he was handsome with his reddish-brown fur and a mane as black as midnight.

"This is Milkshake. He's a twelve-year-old Morgan and as gentle as they come."

Hannah stayed several feet back. "He doesn't have a saddle on. Am I supposed to ride him bareback?"

"You get points for knowing the term 'bareback.' But you aren't going to ride today. We are going to work on getting to know him and have him trust you."

"Why wouldn't he trust me? What has he heard?"

Maggie laughed.

"Sorry. I make jokes when I'm nervous."

"Quite all right. Milkshake farts when he's nervous." There was that smile again.

"You make jokes too."

"I'm not joking. Best not to make him nervous. It can get very unpleasant."

"Good to know."

Maggie untied the rope but held the horse in place. "Want to come closer and pet him?"

"Not really."

"Work with me here. I've got a hold of him. Come over and stand next to me. You don't have to touch him. Yet. Just get closer."

Hannah inched her way over. Maggie didn't smell like horses or hay, like Hannah thought she might, spending so much time in the barn. She smelled like—Hannah breathed in her scent—strawberries and vanilla. Sweet. For a moment, she forgot there was a horse nearby.

"Good job."

"Yes. I learned to walk when I was a year old. Been getting better ever since."

Maggie ran her hand down the horse's face, stopping just short of his nose. "How are you feeling? Check in with your body. See if there are any signs of anxiety anywhere."

Hannah took a moment to give it some thought. The tightness that was in her chest earlier seemed to have eased up. Maybe it was because Maggie was between her and the horse. "I feel okay."

Maggie took a step back. "And now?"

Still okay. "Fine."

"I'm going to have you touch him. Where do you think you would feel most comfortable doing that?"

"Hawaii. I've always wanted to go to Hawaii."

"I meant where on his body, smart-ass."

"Not his face. He has a mouth there." Hannah wasn't sure she wanted to touch him anywhere.

"Okay. That leaves a whole lot of body left."

"How about on his side? There's nothing there that can bite or kick. I don't think."

"He's not going to bite you. I promise."

Hannah didn't know how Maggie could be so sure. She had no choice but to trust her.

Maggie gently pulled the harness thing, whatever it was called, on the horse's head and turned him so his side was closer to Hannah. "Just lay your hand on him. You don't even have to move it. Baby steps."

Hannah took a deep breath and closed her eyes for a long moment. She opened them, put her hand out in front of her, and took a few small steps toward the horse, stopping just short of touching him. She looked over at Maggie. Maggie nodded and Hannah laid her hand on the horse's side. He didn't move or acknowledge her presence. She didn't know what to expect but thought his fur would feel rough. It was kind of soft, like a short-haired dog. Not bad at all.

"Can you pet him?" Maggie asked.

"Like move my hand?"

Maggie laughed. "Yes. Like move your hand. Like you would pet a cat. Go ahead."

Hannah did it. It wasn't as hard as she thought it would be.

"So?"

"So far, so good. No fainting or throwing up. And no farting. At least not from me. Okay. I touched his fur."

"Hair."

"What?" Hannah asked.

"A horse has hair. Not fur. You did excellent. You touched a horse and didn't die." Maggie couldn't quite believe that Hannah had taken her up on her offer. She also couldn't believe just how scared of horses she really was.

"Thanks for your patience. You must think I'm a big baby."

"Not at all. But I am curious. Cassidy has been involved with horses for a lot of years. How come after all this time you decide you want to learn to ride?"

Hannah lowered her eyes and took several beats to answer. "I felt left out when the two of you went riding. And it seemed like Cassidy would have liked it if I could ride too. That must seem pretty childish."

The one thing she had in common with Cassidy and Hannah wanted to intrude on it. Shit. And here she was helping her. A part of her was pissed. But the other part of her understood. She would probably be feeling insecure in Hannah's shoes too. Besides, at this rate it would probably take Hannah years before she would actually ride a horse.

"I appreciate your honesty," she said instead of telling her how she really felt. Making an enemy of Hannah would just hurt Maggie in the long run. "You know this isn't a competition, right? You have so much with Cassidy. I would never want to interfere with that or try to take it away."

"You have to understand how hard this is for me. And for Cassidy."

"And you have to understand how hard it has been for me. You got to raise my daughter. I missed out on eighteen years of her life." Maggie worked at keeping her voice steady.

"And my biological children were never born."

Okay, so we're going there. "Are you blaming me for that?"

To her surprise, Hannah started to cry. "I don't know what to think or even feel anymore. The life I had planned turned out nothing like I expected. My wife died and now I find out that Cassidy isn't even my child. What the hell?"

Maggie had an urge to comfort her but didn't make a move toward doing it. Hannah had no reason to cry. She *had* Cassidy. Maggie had no one. No partner—not that she needed one—and no child. *Her* life hadn't turned out as she had planned it either.

Maggie refused to feel sorry for Hannah. She had so much more than she did.

Randi chose that moment to show up for work. "Hi, boss. Thought I would get ready—" She stopped when she saw Hannah crying. "Um." Her eyebrows went up a half an inch. "Should I go and…"

Hannah swiped at the tears on her cheeks. "I'm sorry. Maybe this wasn't a good idea." She started toward her car, with Maggie on her heels.

"Hannah, there is no need to stop. If you want to learn to ride, I'm still willing to teach you." Maggie wasn't sure why she was still offering. Maybe she *was* feeling sorry for her.

"How much do I owe you for the lesson?" Hannah wiped a few more errant tears.

"You don't owe me anything. Come back and let's do a little more work today." Maggie wasn't sure why she didn't just let Hannah leave. Maybe she thought it would hurt her chances of forming a relationship with Cassidy. The nicer she was to Hannah, the better. "Please."

Hannah looked at her. She seemed liked she was trying to make a decision. Or maybe she was trying to figure Maggie out.

"You know we are going to have lots of confusing, hurtful moments over this. This situation is just—" Maggie stopped.

"Fucking messed up?"

Maggie laughed. "Yes. That about sums it up. Do you think maybe we could sit down and calmly talk about this? Share what we are going through?"

Hannah nodded.

"Let me go talk to Randi for a minute, have her take care of Milkshake. I'll meet you in the house. Make yourself at home. It's unlocked. I'll be there in a few minutes. Okay?"

Hannah nodded again.

Maggie watched her go into the house before she headed down to the barn.

"What was that all about?" Randi asked as Maggie approached.

"Just two mothers with one kid and a whole lot of emotion." She asked Randi to see to Milkshake, then headed back to the house. She took a deep breath and went inside.

Hannah was leaning back against the kitchen counter.

"Sit. Please. Tea?"

"That would be good. Thank you." Hannah sat.

Maggie put the kettle on to boil, put a couple of tea bags into cups and sat across from Hannah. She waited, but Hannah didn't say anything, so she started. "I know this is hard for both of us. For all of us. I can't imagine being in Cassidy's position. How does she seem to be handling it?"

"To tell you the truth I think she is in denial. Or at least isn't really facing it yet. I'm not getting much out of her."

"Do you think maybe a counselor would be a good idea? I can help pay if that is an issue."

"It's not. I'll talk to her about it."

"Do you think we should go to the fertility clinic and find out how this happened?"

"Do you think they would even be honest with us?"

"If we go in with a lawyer they might."

"Threaten to sue them?"

The tea kettle let out a scream, and Maggie saw Hannah jump. She quickly turned off the stove and finished making the tea and set the cups, along with milk and sugar, on the table.

"I don't want to sue them. Do you?" Maggie said once she sat back down.

"Not really. It would be as if I'm sorry I had Cassidy, and that's not the case."

"I agree. But I would like to know how this could happen and make sure it never happens again." She put a spoonful of sugar in her tea and slowly stirred it, staring into it as if it held the answers they sought.

"You said your biological children were never born. We are assuming your embryos were implanted in me and they didn't take. Is that right?"

Hannah nodded.

"And mine were implanted in you and one took and turned out to be Cassidy. That's something we need to know as well."

"Oh my God. You don't think it's possible there was another woman in the mix-up who got mine?"

Maggie shook her head. "I think that would be very unlikely." She had been thinking a lot about all this in the last several days. In fact, it was pretty much all she could think about. It had been hard to keep her mind on work or lessons. "I feel like I was robbed of my child for her whole life. At the same time, I feel fortunate that she exists in this world and that I know about her and have had the opportunity to spend time with her." Maggie sipped her tea. "I missed out on so much. From singing her nursery rhymes to her high school graduation."

"I know it's not the same, but I can make copies of my photos. And Cassidy was never much into nursery rhymes." Hannah smiled. "I was actually glad about that. I've never been much of a fan either."

"Why is that?"

"Think about it. Let's take 'Three Little Kittens' for example. They lost their mittens and they began to cry."

Maggie nodded. She remembered that one.

"Did their mother try to help them find the mittens or even comfort them? No. She said they were naughty kittens and refused to give them pie. Same thing when they got their mittens soiled. Those kittens were going to grow up and base their self-worth on how well they took care of those damn mittens. What were they even wearing mittens for anyway? They were kittens for God's sake."

Maggie laughed and Hannah smiled at her. She liked Hannah, her humor, and her insight. They weren't enemies. She hoped they could be friends. "I love that. Guess the cradle that falls from the treetop, baby and all wasn't a favorite either?"

"Nope."

Maggie turned serious. "I can't help but think that if she had been…" Maggie took a long moment to think of the right words. "If she had been implanted in me, she might not have survived." She reached across the table and put her hand on top of Hannah's. "And I'm so glad she did."

When Hannah didn't say anything, Maggie continued. "I'm so sorry that the embryos, your embryos, didn't."

Hannah slipped her hand from beneath Maggie's and put it in her lap. The move didn't go unnoticed by Maggie.

Maggie's touch felt good. Too good. Confusingly good. Hannah needed to make the feeling go away so she could think. "I feel the loss of them," Hannah said. "I know it was a long time ago and nothing can change it. Don't get me wrong. Cassidy is my child, biology or not, and I love her with all my heart. But I feel like something was stolen from me. I imagine you feel the same."

"That pretty much sums it up. Hannah, I'm not trying to take Cassidy from you. I only want the opportunity to get to know her. For her to get to know me and my family."

"Your family?" Hannah hadn't even considered the possibility of Cassidy having a whole other family out there. She had been too overwhelmed with just the thought of her having another mother.

"My father, sister, and two nieces. I told my sister about Cassidy and she's been very supportive. I haven't even told my father yet. I wanted to see where this went first. I wasn't sure if you would even let me see Cassidy or if she would want to see me."

"And your mother?" Hannah assumed she had died.

"She left us when I was barely out of diapers. I haven't seen or heard from her since."

Hannah hadn't expected that answer. How could a mother do that to her children? "Oh wow. I'm so sorry."

"So, finding a daughter when I was searching for a mother has kind of messed with my mind some."

"I imagine it would."

"Hannah, I would like to see Cassidy again."

"I assumed you would. I'll talk to her. We'll set something up." She rose. "Thanks for the tea." Hannah glanced at the still full cup. "I'll also check out counselors for Cassidy."

Maggie stood. "Please keep me in the loop. I would really appreciate it."

"Of course."

Maggie was going to be a part of Cassidy's life. There was no way around it.

Hannah's head was swimming on the ride home. So much to think about. Touching the horse wasn't nearly as bad as she had thought it would be. Maggie had been so patient with her. She was still willing to continue with the lessons she'd said. It was something to consider. Crying in front of Maggie was embarrassing. The talk they had cleared up some of her feelings and gave her a better understanding of Maggie's. Maggie touching her hand had been a surprise. A surprise that she offered comfort. A surprise at the reaction her body had to it. A reaction she hadn't had with anyone in a long time. A counselor for Cassidy was a good idea. Round and round her thoughts went and round again.

She was emotionally exhausted by the time she pulled into the driveway. Cassidy wasn't home yet. She took the opportunity to research counselors on her laptop and found one that looked promising. She called to make sure they were accepting new clients. They were. It would be up to Cassidy to make the final decision. Hannah wasn't going to force her. She bookmarked the webpage, closed her computer, and headed upstairs to take a shower.

She was toweling off when she heard Cassidy call to her. She cracked open the bathroom door and yelled, "Be right down."

Cassidy was making herself a sandwich when Hannah entered the kitchen. "Guess you won't want dinner in an hour," she said.

"Why would you even think that? Have you met me? I'll be ready to eat again in like twenty minutes."

"How was work?"

Cassidy set her sandwich on the table and poured herself a glass of juice. "Good. We got a new student today. He's only ten and you would swear he's been riding horses his whole life."

A ten-year-old could ride a horse like an expert and she felt good because she touched a horse today. If a kid could do it, she could do it. Probably. Maybe.

Cassidy sat at the table. "Are you listening, Mom?"

Hannah realized she'd been in her own head. "I am. Kid. Ten. Rode like he was born on a horse."

"Close enough."

"Speaking of being born on a horse—what would you think about seeing a counselor?"

"What? What does that have to do with a horse? Or me for that matter?"

Hannah sat across from her and folded her hands in front of her. "It has to do with the being born part. Being born from the wrong mother." *That didn't come out right.*

"Mom." Hannah could hear the annoyance in her voice.

"That's not what I meant. Finding out about Maggie was a shock. To all of us. Maggie and I think it might be helpful if you had someone to talk to. A professional."

"Maggie? Since when does Maggie get a say in my life?"

"She doesn't. This is me asking you. I think it would be a good idea."

"Why?"

"Because you really haven't talked to me about it, and you seem to be holding it all in. Have you talked to anyone about it?"

"Oh my God, no. It's embarrassing. The last thing I need is for my friends to think I'm a freak."

"Is that what you think?"

Cassidy pushed her plate away from her. "What would you call it? How many times do you think something like this happens? One in a million? One in ten million? Never except for me? Yeah. That makes me a freak."

Hannah knew Cassidy wasn't taking it well, but she had no idea it was this bad. "Oh, honey. You are not a freak. Far from it. You have a mother who raised you and loves you. You have another person out there, Maggie, who wants to get to know you and love you." Hannah let out a long breath. "Yes, this is an unusual situation, but it doesn't make you anything other than what you have always been."

"And what's that?" Cassidy's voice softened but still held an edge of anger.

"A kind, smart, beautiful young lady."

Cassidy bit her bottom lip. "It's just so much, Mom. It's hard to accept."

"Even after meeting Maggie and seeing the similarities? Your love of horses for example."

"It just feels so mixed up in my mind. How could a woman that I've never met or didn't even know existed be my mother?"

"I'm your mother and always will be. But she missed out on having a child. You're her chance to make that right." Hannah felt like she was pleading Maggie's case instead of helping her daughter. She wasn't sure why.

"That's not my problem."

"It's not. And you don't have to worry about that part. Forget that I even said it. But do you see my point? A counselor might be able to help you figure some of this out. Help with your feelings. It's not that I'm not willing to listen and help you through it the best I can, but a professional might be able to offer insight that I can't. I'm just too close to the situation. What do you think?"

"I guess."

"You guess what?"

"I guess I could see someone. Knowing you, you've already been online and found someone."

"I guess you've met me. I have."

"Female I hope."

"Of course."

Cassidy pulled the plate closer and nibbled on the edge of her sandwich. "Did you make me an appointment?"

"Of course not. I may be pushy, but I'm not that pushy. I will though if you want me to."

"Just forward the site and I'll do it."

Hannah knew Cassidy well enough to know if she said she would, she would follow through. "Do you want me to go with you to the first appointment?"

Cassidy shook her head. "I'm not a little kid anymore, Mom. I can handle it."

"Sometimes I can't handle the fact that you're not a little kid anymore. Sometimes I can't believe you've graduated from high school. I feel like I'm barely old enough to be out of school myself."

Cassidy laughed. It was a welcomed sound that Hannah had missed the last week. "You had your twentieth high school reunion a few years ago. How can you feel like you're barely old enough to be out of school?"

"Hey. You're only as old as you feel."

"So, you feel like you're what, like twenty?" Cassidy took a decent-sized bite of her food. A good sign that she was calming down.

"Why yes. Yes, I do. Sometimes. Not often. But sometimes. Mostly I mentally feel twenty. My body likes to remind me that I'm in my forties—low forties. A lot."

"I'm sorry, Mom."

Hannah was confused. "For what?"

"For being a problem."

"What are you talking about?"

"If it wasn't for me, you wouldn't be going through any of this."

Hannah got up and gave Cassidy a hug from behind. "You, my love, have nothing to be sorry for. I wouldn't trade you for anything."

Cassidy looked up at Hannah.

"For anything," Hannah repeated. "I love you." One way or another she was going to help her daughter get through this. A big part of her wanted to help Maggie get through it too, but she wasn't sure why.

Hannah sent a text to her two sisters and her mother asking if they could meet up at her mom's house after work the next day. They went back and forth until all four had agreed on a time. She told Cassidy that she was going to let them know about Maggie and asked her if she wanted to join them. She didn't.

"What's going on?" her mother asked once they were all sitting in lawn chairs on the back deck. "Cassidy's not pregnant, is she?"

Hannah laughed more out of nervousness than because she thought it was funny. That's all they needed to complicate things even further. "No, Mom."

Sarah gave her a knowing look and nodded. It was just the encouragement Hannah needed to get the words out. She explained about the DNA test, finding out about Maggie, and them meeting her.

"Well, I'll be goddamned," her mother said. "That is the craziest thing I've ever heard. What are you going to do about it?"

"What can I do? It's not like we are going to fight over custody. We're kind of taking baby steps to figure this out."

"How is Cassidy doing with all this?" her sister Linda asked. "And you?"

"I think we are both in shock. Cassidy is having a hard time of course. It would probably be better if you don't ask her. At least not right now. I feel…" she paused, trying to put into words all the confusing, scary, heartbreaking emotions that had been running through her. "I feel like I'm not surprised. Not that I expected this. But Cassidy doesn't look like anyone in our family. It breaks my heart to find out that I'm not her biological mother. But I'm her mother in every other sense of the word."

"Does this woman—what was her name—Marge, what does she have to say?" her mother asked.

"It's Maggie and she is just as surprised as we are. She doesn't have any children even though she tried. So, finding out about Cassidy is like a dream come true, as well as a nightmare, I would imagine."

"I can't image what you all are going through," Linda said. "What do you need from us?"

"Nothing really. I just wanted to let you know. We don't want a lot of attention around this, so for now I would appreciate if you didn't tell anyone else—except your kids and husbands, of course. And ask them not to repeat it. Maggie seems like a reasonable person. I don't think she is going to do anything crazy or stupid." At least Hannah hoped she wouldn't.

Chapter Eight

"Maggie sent me a text and asked me to come over," Cassidy said to Hannah over breakfast.

"I'm not surprised. She wants to get to know you. Did you answer her?" Hannah poured cereal into her bowl. Not the healthiest choice, but she was running late.

"Not yet. I really don't want to go alone. I know I'm being a big baby, but I'm just not ready yet. Will you go with me?"

Hannah poured the last of the milk into her bowl. It only covered about half of the cereal. She'd asked Cassidy on numerous occasions to let her know when they were running low on something. Cassidy rarely remembered. "You're going to have to ask Maggie if she is okay with that. I don't think the invitation included me. It's only polite to ask."

Cassidy pulled her phone from her front pocket—breaking the *no phone at the table* rule—and typed.

Hannah shook her head but didn't say anything.

Cassidy's phone pinged almost immediately. She read the text and looked up at Hannah. "She said it was fine."

"Wow. That was fast."

"Does Thursday work for you?"

"Yeah, if it's after two."

Cassidy typed. "Okay. Thursday at three." Cassidy set her phone down and picked up her fork. "Thanks, Mom."

"For what?"

"For going with me. I know it's probably not your favorite thing to do."

"No problem." And it wasn't. She actually looked forward to seeing Maggie again, which kind of shocked her. But there was something about her that drew Hannah in. She seemed like a caring person. She certainly didn't push when it came to Cassidy. Hannah suspected that someone else in her position might make life very hard for them.

Hannah's phone pinged. She broke her own rule and looked at the text. To her surprise it was from Maggie.

Maggie: *I'm sure you know I just set up a get together with you and Cassidy. Thank you for being agreeable to this. Thought maybe you could come out before that and we could work with Milkshake again. Tuesday?*

Hannah smiled. That was so thoughtful, especially since Hannah had almost stormed out the last time.

Cassidy put her bowl in the dishwasher and grabbed her backpack from the hook by the door. "Bye, Mom. I won't be home for dinner. I'm going to Gabby's after work. I've got extra clothes, so I'll change over there after teaching."

"Don't change. I like you just the way you are."

Cassidy smiled at the old joke. "Bye, Mom."

"Bye, love." Another dinner alone. Oh well. It was going to be a pizza night ordered from the place around the corner. Netflix— but no chill. "Okay, honey. Love you."

"Love you too. Oh, and I made an appointment with that counselor," Cassidy called as she slipped out the door.

Hannah was glad. She hoped it would help Cassidy accept the curveball life had thrown at them. She took a minute and reread Maggie's text. She hadn't been sure if she should continue with the lessons, but Maggie was willing, so why not.

Hannah: *Are you sure it's no trouble?*

Maggie: *It's no trouble. I see it more as a challenge.*

Hannah: *Because I'm such a wuss?*

Hannah watched as the dots appeared indicating that Maggie was responding. The dots disappeared, and then reappeared.

Maggie: *I was going to say no, but yeah. It's 'cause you're a wuss. I have never met anyone with as much fear of horses as you have. I taught a guy that fell off a horse and the horse accidently stepped on him, breaking his leg, and he had less fear than you do.*

Hannah: *Oh my God!!!! That story did nothing to reduce my fear. In fact, now I'm not sure I want to go near another horse. EVER!!!!!*

There was a long pause before Maggie answered and Hannah wondered if Maggie was giving up on her.

Maggie: *Oh yeah. I made that story up. Lied through my teeth.*

Hannah: *You did not. You're lying through your teeth now.*

Maggie: *How did you know?*

Hannah: *I can see it in your eyes.*

Maggie: *You can see me through texting? Damn, you're talented.*

Hannah: *Or I'm stalking you and I'm outside your house looking in your window.*

Maggie: *Well come on in and I'll make you a cup of tea.*

Hannah: *Can't today. I'm crawling back to my car now. Have to head to work.*

Maggie: *How about that lesson on Tuesday? And by the way. That guy didn't fall off the horse during one of my lessons. He did that all on his own. And that's the truth.*

Hannah agreed to another lesson.

Maggie wasn't sure why that made her so happy, but it did. She reread their text messages and laughed again. Maggie appreciated Hannah's sense of humor. She slipped her phone in her pocket, grabbed her work gloves, and headed down to the barn. Randi wasn't due for a couple more hours, but Maggie like the quiet of the morning in the barn alone. She led the horses out of their stalls to the field so they could graze, and she set about mucking the stalls.

The wheelbarrow was full, but years of pushing it had built up the muscles Maggie needed to wheel it about twenty yards behind the barn. She dumped it with very little effort. The large pile would get picked up on Friday and be brought to a local organic farm where it would get processed into fertilizer. Maggie liked the thought of making the world a little more organic.

She was just coming around the side of the barn with the now empty wheelbarrow when she spotted her sister, Jean, walking toward her. Maggie waved.

"Hey there. I had the day off so I thought I would stop by and see how you're doing?"

"Checking up on me to see how it went with Cassidy and her mother?"

"You know me well."

Maggie laughed. "Yeah, I do. Let me wash up a bit and we can chat."

Jean sat on the glider swing on the porch and Maggie went inside. She bypassed the kitchen sink in favor of using the bathroom and the larger hand towels.

She stuck her head out the side door a few minutes later. "Want tea or coffee?"

"I'm all coffeed out," Jean said. "Three cups this morning. I'm fine. I don't need anything."

"I would be shaking like a leaf if I drank that much," Maggie said as she sat next to Jean and set the glider swaying, pushing off the floor with her foot.

"That's a stupid saying. Leaves don't shake. You would be shaking like a vibrator," Jean said.

Maggie shook her head. She never knew what was going to be coming out of her sister's mouth. "I believe I would be vibrating in that case."

"Have you told Dad yet? About Cassidy?"

"No. If you remember, he wasn't happy about me trying to get pregnant..." Maggie made air quotes with her fingers. "Without a man."

"I thought he got over that."

"I think he was relieved when I didn't end up pregnant and didn't try again. I'm not sure how he's going to react. And I want to see where this goes before I tell him."

"I think he'll be understanding. He's come a long way in the last dozen years."

Maggie tilted her head. "Yeah. Maybe."

"Tell me about your visit. I can't believe you haven't called me to tell me how it went."

"I guess I needed some time to process it. It went well, I think. Cassidy seems like a lovely young woman. Hannah has done a great job raising her. And get this." Maggie put her hand on her sister's knee for emphasis. "She rides horses and even gives riding lessons to younger kids." Maggie was surprised at how much pride she felt. Her genes had obviously made an impact on Cassidy.

"Wow. That's amazing. How did you feel seeing her?"

"It was weird. Great. But weird. She looks a lot like I did at that age. She's my kid, but she's a stranger. And she seems to be having a hard time with this."

"Of course, she is. What kid wouldn't? Are you?"

"Having a hard time?"

Jean nodded.

Maggie thought about it. Hard wasn't the right word for it. Pissed? Maybe. Disappointed? Definitely. Happy that Cassidy existed in the world? Absolutely. "I wouldn't say that. There are a whole lot of emotions. I'm hopeful that Cassidy will want to have a relationship with me and at the same time there is a part of me that worries she won't. She's kind of hard to read, but I've only met her once, so I'm sure it will take time."

"And her mother—the woman who raised her?"

"Mother is the right word. She is her mother in every sense of the word except for biology. And as we know from personal experience, biology doesn't make someone a mother. If it did Mom would still be around." Their father had done the best he could, but he was dealing with his own hurt from his wife up and leaving. The note she left said only *I can't do it anymore.* Jean, being seven years older than Maggie, was the closest thing to a mother she had. She was grateful for her.

"Well, you didn't leave Cassidy. She can't blame you for not raising her."

"No, but she can resent me for showing up and disrupting her life. I have to tread lightly."

"You didn't answer me. Her mother? Hannah? Do you think she wants to keep Cassidy from you?"

"She actually seems to understand what this is like for me. We had a really good talk the other day. This is just as much of a shock to her as it is to me."

"What is she like?"

"She's pretty, dark blond hair, bright eyes—blue. Fair complexion. Short. Well, shorter than me, anyways." Yeah, very pretty.

Jean just stared at her for a beat or two.

"What?"

"That's quite the description. I was asking more about her personality." She paused again. "If I didn't know any better, I would say you're attracted to her."

Maggie thought about it for a moment before answering. "Under different circumstances I probably would be."

"And under these circumstances you're not?"

Maggie tapped her foot against the porch deck before pushing off, sending the glider swinging again. "I can't be. It would be a bad idea."

"Why?"

Maggie tilted her head, looking into Jean's eyes. "Why? You don't think this is confusing enough for Cassidy without me hitting on her mother?"

"I'm not telling you to hit on her. That sounds crass. But if you're attracted to her, then what's the harm in getting to know her. Maybe she feels the same."

"She doesn't."

Maggie stopped the swing and stood. "Let's go in and get some iced tea. I'm parched." She started in, not waiting for Jean to stand up. Once inside, she poured two glasses of tea, put a spoonful of sugar in one glass, and stirred.

Jean followed her in, grabbed the tray of ice from the freezer, and added some to each glass. She took the one with the sugar and leaned a hip against the counter. "So?"

"What?"

"So how do you know she—Hannah—doesn't feel the same?"

Maggie took sip of her tea before answering. "How could she? I showed up in her and Cassidy's life and turned it upside down. I'm just glad she doesn't seem to hate me."

"Let's go back to the original question."

Maggie raised an eyebrow, waiting for Jean to remind her of what that was.

"What is she like—personality-wise?"

"She's nice. Good sense of humor. Good mother. I don't know much more." Not that she didn't want to. She had the desire to get to know her almost as much as she wanted to get to know Cassidy. And it was only partially because she was the one who raised Cassidy.

Randi led Milkshake out of the barn and tethered him to the fence rail. Another trip into the barn and she returned with the mounting block, which she placed next to the horse. He was already saddled.

"Thanks," Maggie said. "You okay handling things around here while I work with Hannah?"

Randi shook her head sarcastically—if there was such a thing. "I've only been working here for years. I'm pretty sure I've got the routine down by now."

Maggie felt foolish. It *was* a stupid question. For some reason she was nervous about seeing Hannah again. The talk with her sister got her to examining her feelings for Hannah. And she wasn't happy to realize how much she liked her. True, she barely knew her. But apparently that didn't matter. She needed to shelve these feelings. They would only cause her trouble.

"I've got this." Randi's words broke into her thoughts.

"I know. I'm sorry. Hannah should—" She looked up in time to see Hannah walking toward them. "And here she comes now." Looking as good as ever in her jeans and a T-shirt just tight enough to show off her assets. *Stop it.*

A big smile was plastered across Hannah's face as she let herself in the gate.

Maggie was sure her smile matched. "Hi there. I hope that smile means you're not as scared today."

Hannah's smile faded and Maggie was sorry she'd said that.

"Hi, Hannah," Randi said. She looked from Hannah to Maggie. "Work to do," she said and disappeared into the barn.

Maggie wondered what she was thinking with that look. She turned her attention back to Hannah. Some reassurance was in order here. "You did great last time. We'll have a good day."

Hannah laughed. "I touched a horse. Don't know how great that makes me."

"It's more than you'd have done a couple of weeks ago. Give yourself some credit."

"Oh yeah. Okay. Credit given." Hannah had stopped at least a yard from Milkshake.

Maggie crooked a finger and did that *come closer* motion. "If you're ready, let's start where we left off. Come here and lay your hand on Milkshake's side."

Hannah swallowed hard. It didn't kill her last time to touch the horse. It wouldn't kill her now. She crossed the gap between them and placed her hand gently on the horse. This time the sensation felt familiar. She breathed a sigh of relief. The breath in that followed it smelled slightly of horse and something else. Vanilla. And? Hannah breathed in again. Sandalwood. She doubted Milkshake had perfume or more likely essential oils on. The pleasant smell was, no doubt, coming from Maggie.

"See. You didn't even hesitate that time. Progress." She had Hannah stay in that spot for a couple of minutes, encouraging her to pet the horse for longer this time. Feel his coat. Feel him breathe. "Come on over here and touch his mane."

Hannah hesitated only a moment. She knew if she thought about it too long, she would get anxious. The mane felt different from the hair on his side did. It was more like human hair. Like the long hair on a beautiful woman. It was something Hannah hadn't felt in a very long while. It wasn't until that moment that she realized how much she had missed that feeling. She glanced at Maggie's long dark hair, pulled back into a ponytail. Hannah's face flushed with heat.

"Doing okay? You're turning a bit red in the face there. Need to back away?"

Hannah shook away the thought of touching Maggie's hair. She prayed the blush would go away as well. "I'm fine." She stroked the mane, remembering that it belonged to a horse and at the same time trying to forget that fact. She had never been this close to one before. It wasn't as horrible as she had imagined. Of course, Maggie standing right next to her, holding the rope so the horse didn't turn his head toward Hannah, helped.

"Think you can work your way up to his nose? Stroke right here." Maggie ran her hand from between the horse's eyes to his nose.

"That's really close to his mouth."

Maggie ran her hand under the horse's chin and across his mouth. "He is as gentle as they come. He won't bite you. I promise." She stepped to the side.

Hannah assumed it was to give her more room. But she seemed too far away for safety. "Can you move closer? I would feel better if you did." Hannah knew she was being a baby. She was trying to be brave but falling a little short. "Please?"

Maggie took a step to the side. Still not close enough.

"A little more," Hannah said.

Maggie moved again.

Hannah stepped around to Milkshake's face. Maggie was so close that the hairs on Hannah's arms stood up. She wasn't sure if the anxiety she felt was from being so close to a horse or so close to Maggie. Probably both.

Hannah put her hand up but couldn't bring herself to actually touch Milkshake's face. She froze. Maggie placed her hand on Hannah's and looked at her, silently asking a question. Hannah nodded her response and Maggie gently pushed Hannah's hand forward until it rested on the horse. She slipped her fingers between Hannah's as she pulled Hannah's hand down with hers, stroking the horse's face.

It was confusing. The soft cool texture of the horse's hair on her fingertips and the warm, soft texture of Maggie's hand on hers. She was surprised at just how soft it was. She would have thought it would be rough and calloused from the type of work she did.

Maggie brought Hannah's hand back up and together they stroked Milkshake's nose again. Hannah repeated the movement on her own when Maggie removed her hand. Hannah missed its warmth, despite the heat of the day.

Milkshake made a sudden sneezing sound, shaking his head as he did it, frightening Hannah. She stepped back so quickly that she lost her balance. Maggie's arm was around her in an instant, stopping her from falling. Hannah reached out, and before she knew what was happening, she had her arms wrapped around Maggie.

Not only was the position she found herself in surprising, she was just as surprised that Maggie didn't pull away. They stayed with their arms around each other for what seemed like an hour but was probably way less than a minute. Was it her imagination, or did Maggie look longingly at her lips, if only for a second? Hannah chalked it up to her overactive imagination and to the fact that she had glanced at Maggie's lips with the urge to kiss them. To see if they were as soft as her hands were. Probably softer.

Hannah found her senses before she had a chance to do something stupid. She extracted herself and took a careful step backward. She pulled her focus away from Maggie and those lips—oh, those lips—and put it once again on the large animal in front of her.

"I should have warned you about that. My fault," Maggie said. "Are you all right?"

Hannah nodded. She willed her racing heartbeat to slow down. "Why did he do that? Was that a sneeze?"

"He does that when he likes something. It's a sign of pleasure. He likes having his face stroked."

"He scared the shit out of me." Hannah put her hand over her mouth. "Sorry."

"Quite all right. I've heard that word a time or two. May have even said it a million times or more."

Hannah smiled. Maggie had a way of breaking the tension.

"Feel free to use even stronger words if you need to. Nothing wrong with a good fuck now and then." Maggie blushed. "I mean saying the word, not the act…" Her face turned an even darker shade of red. "Shit."

Hannah laughed. "Um. Okay. I think I get your drift."

"I'll stop before I make a fool of myself."

"Might be too late for that."

"Hey."

"What is—food for horses, Alex?"

"Ah. A *Jeopardy* fan, huh?"

"I've been known to answer an answer with a question." Hannah thought about what she said for a moment. "Yeah. That's right," she said to herself as much as she said it to Maggie.

"Ready to go for a ride on Milkshake?" Maggie asked, apparently trying to get them back on track.

"What is a crazy idea, Alex?" Hannah said.

Maggie shook her head. "You're a little crazy, aren't you?"

"You're just now figuring that out?"

"I didn't want to say anything until I had proof." Maggie smiled that bright smile of hers.

Hannah tried not to melt. She couldn't think of a snappy comeback. So unlike her, but Maggie's smile had landed on her heart. Or was it an area much lower? Now was not the time for such thoughts—or feelings.

"I'm just kidding you know," Maggie said.

"I know. But you're right. I'm a little crazy. It's more fun than being insane."

"Been there. Done that. Bought the T-shirt." Maggie waved a hand toward Milkshake. "I was hoping we could get up on him today. Maybe take a little walk around the corral. I'll be leading him the whole way. You just have to sit there."

Hannah hadn't expected to start riding yet. It had been hard enough touching the horse. Maggie seemed to think she was ready. She wasn't so sure. Looking like a fool trying to get up in a saddle that was so high up wasn't on her calendar for today.

"I have a mounting block set up already. It makes it much easier to get up and into the saddle," Maggie said as if reading Hannah's mind. "It's on the other side here." She pointed around the horse.

Hannah bent down and looked under the horse. Sure enough, there were steps on the other side. That *would* make it easier. But there was still the fact that she would be sitting on a horse to contend with.

"Ready?" Maggie laid her hand on Hannah's arm.

An electrical charge ran through her at the contact. *Shit. Stop it, body. Not now. Not with her.* She swallowed hard before answering. "You promise you won't let go?"

"I promise. I haven't lost a student yet. You can trust me."

As scared as she was, Hannah *did* trust her. "He's not going to sneeze again, is he? Or fart?"

"Only if he gets excited or anxious, and we'll make sure he doesn't do either of those things."

"What if I tell you I'm still scared?"

Maggie gave Hannah's arm a gentle squeeze. "It's okay to feel fear. Just don't let it control you."

"Great advice from someone who has probably never felt fear in her life."

"Oh, I've known fear. One of the things I feared most in this world came to fruition and I survived. That's how I know fear can't beat us."

Hannah suspected that she was talking about the failed in vitro procedure. "I'm sorry." It was all she could think to say.

"No need. Now let's get your butt up in that saddle."

Hannah started around the back of the horse when Maggie stopped her. "Let's have you walk around the front of Milkshake."

"Oh. Shit. Right. I don't want to get kicked."

Maggie laughed. "Milkshake wouldn't kick you. He's never done anything like that. There's a specific way you walk around the back of a horse to let them know you're there. But, we won't worry about that today. I want you to walk around the front because when you mount, you are actually *facing* the back of the horse. You are going to turn the stirrup around to put your foot in it. Then you take a big hop and swing your leg over." She stepped closer to the horse's face so Hannah could go around her.

"You make it sound so easy."

"It is easy."

Hannah hesitated when she got to the steps. "How do I do this again?"

Maggie talked her through each step until Hannah was sitting on the horse. Actually sitting on a horse. Damn, it was high. She held on to the horn, like Maggie told her to. Maybe too tightly. Her knuckles seemed to be turning white. She let up a little but kept her grip firm.

"I'm going to walk him. We won't go fast. It's important to go with the movement of the horse. Don't fight it."

Hannah wasn't sure she understood but nodded anyway. The saddle felt a little hard under her butt, and when Maggie started Milkshake moving it reminded Hannah of getting a piggyback ride from her dad when she was little. It was strange being up so high on something that was moving. As promised, Maggie went around the corral at a very slow pace, and Hannah was grateful. She quickly realized what Maggie meant by fighting the movement. Her instinct was to move her body the opposite way the horse moved. She found she was much more stable if she went with the movement and let it happen.

"How you doing up there?" Maggie asked.

"Okay. I'm still alive. That's a plus."

"No farting?"

Hannah laughed. "No comment."

They circled the corral three times and ended up where they started. Hannah followed Maggie's directions to dismount and took the hand Maggie offered to help her down the stairs.

"Normally, I would have my student walk the horse around to help him cool off. I don't think Milkshake worked up a sweat today so we're okay skipping it."

"I think I worked up a sweat. Should I walk around to cool down?" Hannah asked.

"How did you work up a sweat just sitting there?"

Hannah laughed. "Anxiety will do that to you."

"Were you really that scared?"

Hannah thought about it for a few moments. "I was to begin with. But I guess that went away after a little while. You really help with that."

"How so?"

"You just have a calm about you. It seems to seep into me by osmosis."

"Good to know. Next time you are going to learn how to saddle Milkshake and then how to take the saddle off after the lesson. I think you've done enough today, so we'll have Randi do it."

Hannah didn't object. She'd offered to pay Maggie for the last lesson and Maggie refused it. But she felt like she owed her something for her time. "Can I take you out to dinner to repay you for the lesson?" At least that way she got to spend more time with her. A bad idea, her brain screamed. She decided to ignore it.

Maggie hesitated. It wasn't a date. It was dinner with the woman who raised her daughter. So what if she found that woman appealing? It didn't mean anything. "You really don't have to do that."

"If I *had* to do it, I probably wouldn't want to." Hannah smiled and her face lit up. Like sexy lit up. Very. Sexy. "That didn't come out right. I know I don't *have* to do it. I *want* to do it. You have to eat, right?"

"Yeah. I eat. Sometimes two or three times a day."

"Then let me buy you something to eat as my way of saying thank you. Please."

"Okay. If you're sure it's no trouble."

"Cassidy said she was hanging out with a friend after work and she usually doesn't come home till late. So, it's not only no trouble, but you would be doing me a favor. I eat dinner alone way too often these days."

"Well, when you put it that way, how can I refuse?"

"You can't. Good. Where can we go with me smelling like a horse?"

"You don't smell like a horse." *You smell like*—Maggie sniffed as discreetly as she could. *Honeysuckle*. She'd noticed it earlier but hadn't taken the time to decipher what it was. "We can go anywhere you want. I'm not fussy. You think about it while I bring Milkshake to Randi." Maggie walked Milkshake back to the barn while Hannah waited.

"How did it go?" Randi asked as Maggie handed her the lead.

"Much better than last time. She's actually doing good for someone with so much fear."

Randi ran her hand over Milkshake's side. "How could anyone be afraid of such a magnificent creature?" She nuzzled her face into his neck and rubbed behind his ears.

He did that sneezing sound and movement that had made Hannah jump. She'd practically leaped into Maggie's arms. And Maggie was hesitant to admit it, even to herself, that she liked it. Liked being so close to her. Liked being in her arms. Liked being her protector—even if there wasn't anything she really needed protection from.

"Can you take care of him, put the mounting block away, and then let him run for a little while in the back fence with the other horses?"

"Of course."

"I'm heading out to dinner with Hannah. I don't think I'll be gone long. You can take off whenever you want. I'll take care of everything else when I get back."

"Dinner? With Hannah?"

"Don't sound too surprised. I eat dinner."

"Yeah, but you don't usually eat dinner with beautiful women."

Maggie wasn't about to admit how beautiful she thought Hannah was. "Hey. I've eaten dinner with you. You're beautiful."

"Ha. I'll take the compliment, but I don't consider myself much more than cute. And I'm not available," Randi said.

"Stop. It's dinner. Not a date." She usually didn't mind Randi's good-natured teasing, but this was different. Randi was going to a place with the joke that Maggie didn't want to go. Or even think about. Although trying not to think about it was starting to be a problem. "Gotta get going. I'll see you in the morning."

"You got it, boss."

Maggie gave her a look that said all was okay between them. Randi smiled. Message received. She headed out of the barn and found Hannah right where she had left her.

"Ready?" Hannah asked.

"Should I change first?" Maggie looked down at her clothes. Jeans and a light green T-shirt. Not fancy, but at least they were clean.

"No. I like you just the way you are."

Hannah's answer took Maggie by surprise and it must have shown on her face.

"Sorry. That's a joke between Cassidy and me. Anytime one of asks if we should change, that's our stock answer."

"Oh. Cute." So, Hannah wasn't saying that she liked her. Not that Maggie thought she *didn't* like her. *God, I'm being ridiculous. Pull your head out of your ass. Assume your clothes are fine and go out to dinner with this woman.* This very attractive, funny, kind woman.

"No. You look fine. We don't have to go somewhere fancy." Hannah paused. "Unless you want to."

"Nope. Casual is fine. Preferred in fact."

"Good. Are you ready?"

"Yep. Want me to drive?"

"I'm not afraid to drive. Just to ride." She smiled.

"Afraid to ride in a car or just horses?"

"Just horses."

They made a quick stop at the house to wash their hands and headed to Hannah's car.

"You did great today. How do you feel?"

"It wasn't as bad as I thought it would be."

"That good, huh?"

"You're a great teacher. I can't say I'm over all my fear, but I did more than I thought I could do."

"If it means anything, I'm proud of you. I know how scary it was for you."

Hannah put a hand over her heart. "Aw. Thank you. That does mean a lot to me."

The sincerity and gesture surprised Maggie. "You really are doing great. Have you told Cassidy that you're taking lessons?"

Hannah put the car in gear and backed out onto the street. "Not yet," she said as soon as she was facing forward again. "I kind of want to surprise her. And…" She strung the word out. "If I end up chickening out, she won't know I failed."

"You won't fail. I am more than happy to keep going until you are riding like a champion."

Hannah gave her a sideways glance. "Champion? I'll be happy to just be able to trot on a horse without falling off. Is that the right word? Trot?"

Maggie couldn't help but laugh.

"Not the right word?"

"I'm sorry. I'm not laughing at you. It's the right word. It was just funny the way you said it."

"I speak-a da funny?"

Maggie laughed again. "Yes. You speak-a da funny. But I like it."

"I like when you laugh. So, I guess that's good."

Yeah. They could be friends. Maggie was sure of it. Who would have thought it?

"Oh yeah. Remind me when we get to the restaurant. I brought pictures for you. Cassidy when she was growing up. I made a DVD too with videos of her. Most are just short clips that I took with my phone so they may not be too good."

Maggie felt tears spring to her eyes. She swiped at the ones that fled and traveled down her cheek.

It didn't escape Hannah's notice. "Hey. Don't cry."

"That was so nice of you. Thank you. I can't wait to see them." More tears.

They were quiet on the rest of the drive to the restaurant. It was a comfortable silence, something Maggie didn't feel with too many people. She usually felt the need to talk or at least play music to fill the empty air. But that was the thing. The air never felt empty with Hannah. It felt *full*, even with no sound.

"Is this place okay?" Hannah asked as she pulled into the parking lot.

"Perfect." The Maple View. More of a diner than a restaurant, but the food was good and the atmosphere causal. She wouldn't feel underdressed. "I've been here with my sister. Great choice. Have you been here before?"

"No. I did a Google search this morning. It had a good rating on Yelp."

So, dinner had been Hannah's plan even before their lesson. That warmed Maggie's heart. She refused to let it warm anything else.

The place was small, quaint, charming. Several booths lined the wall, with tall windows, complete with shades to keep the sun's rays at bay if needed. A handful of tables were scattered about, and the counter had old-fashioned stools reminiscent of those 1950s TV shows.

They were seated immediately, and it wasn't long before they had their drinks and dinners ordered. Hannah pulled a legal-sized envelope out of her purse, thick with what Maggie assumed were photos of Cassidy. Maggie accepted it as if she had been handed a million dollars. But it was worth so much more than that to her. It was priceless.

The photos seemed to be in order and started with pictures of baby Cassidy still in the hospital. "Is this Teri?" Maggie asked, showing Hannah a picture of the infant being held by someone other than Hannah.

"Yes. She was so happy that day."

Maggie looked at each photo, took in the child's face, expression, and gestures—and the moment caught in time that was denied to her. She gently set them on the table as if they were made of crystal or glass. Hannah, every so often, volunteered some tidbit or story about Cassidy related to a photograph Maggie was holding.

Maggie's feelings were a jumble of contradictions. Happy and sad at the same time. And grateful. Grateful that Hannah was kind enough to share. She had missed out on so much and that broke her heart all over again.

Their food arrived just as Maggie reached the end of the pile. "Thank you. I really appreciate this."

"Of course. Oh, and here." Hannah reached into her purse, pulled out a DVD, and handed it to Maggie. "Like I said, the quality of the video isn't the best. If you don't have a DVD player, it will work in your computer."

Maggie knew what she would be doing tonight. Good thing she had a new box of tissues at the ready. She had the urge to give Hannah a kiss to say thank you. Or just to kiss her.

"Thank you so much for everything, the dinner, the company, the pictures. Especially the pictures," Maggie said once they were back at her place. "Would you like to come in for a glass of wine?" The chores could wait a little longer. Maggie was reluctant to let the time with Hannah end.

"That would be nice. Cassidy probably won't be home for a couple more hours at least. Not that I *have* to be home with her. I just don't want her asking where I've been. I want it to be a surprise when I can actually ride a horse."

"I get it."

Hannah followed Maggie inside, glad to be able to spend a little more time with her. She had really enjoyed their time together today—the dinner more than the horse riding. If you could call it riding when all she did was sit there while Maggie did all the work.

"I have red or white," Maggie said. "What is your pleasure?"

Pleasure? Nope. Brain not going there. Body either. "Um. Whichever, really. I like both."

"Then white it is." Maggie wiped out the wine glasses, and Hannah suspected she didn't use them too often. "I have a firepit behind the house. We can sit out there if that works for you. Not too many bugs this time of year."

Romantic. Stop. "Sure, that would be nice."

The sun was just starting to go down when they made their way outside, wine glasses in hand. Hannah sat in the Adirondack chair while Maggie lit the fire. The sky was ablaze with color. The blue giving way to pinks and yellows. The air wasn't quite chilly yet, and the fire was more for atmosphere than warmth. It roared to life and danced about in the metal ring that contained it.

"You must be an expert because I've never seen a fire start so quickly and so completely," Hannah said. "You seem to know your stuff."

"Yeah, I know stuff. I'm a stuff-knower." She laughed. "Actually, it's all in how you stack the wood. They called me the fire starter when I was young and we would go camping."

"Sounds like a dangerous name."

"Oh, I can be dangerous when I want to be."

Hannah had no doubt. She was already proving to be dangerous to Hannah's libido. A libido that hadn't been awakened in quite some time.

A silence settled in around them, interrupted from time to time by the croaking of a nearby frog or the symphony of crickets that serenaded them.

"I had a very nice time today," Maggie said, breaking the silence.

"Me too. I'm glad you agreed to have dinner with me. And this wine…" Hannah held up her glass. "Is wonderful."

Maggie grabbed the bottle that was next to her and tilted it, silently asking Hannah if she wanted a refill. She held her glass out for Maggie to fill. Two glasses were usually her limit, and tonight, with Maggie so close and her feelings—or was it her hormones—running wild, two was *definitely* going to be the limit.

The last thing she needed was to say, or worse yet, do something stupid. Something she couldn't take back. Maggie was interested in getting to know Cassidy. Hannah was just along for the ride. She was sure Maggie had no real interest in her.

Hannah was a little light-headed by the time she finished her second glass. She knew it would pass in short order, but driving wasn't going to happen until then.

"Tell me about your family," Maggie said. "Have you told them yet about…" She paused. "About me and the mix-up?"

"I told my two sisters and my mom, yes. I haven't told anyone else, and Cassidy hasn't either. My dad died a few years ago."

"I'm so sorry."

"Thanks. I didn't get a lot of feedback from them. I don't think they knew quite how to respond."

"I can understand that. There's no playbook for this."

"There isn't, is there? Guess we are all just flying by the seat of our pants. Cassidy made an appointment with a counselor by the way. I think it will help."

"I'm so glad."

Hannah shook her head. "Did you tell your family?"

"I've talked to my sister, Jean, about it. She has been a great sounding board. I haven't told my father yet." She poured more wine into her own glass.

"Can I ask why?"

"He wasn't supportive when I wanted a baby in the first place. Or supportive of me being gay for that matter. He said he didn't *approve* of my lifestyle." She made air quotes.

"Ouch."

"Yeah. I told him that if by lifestyle he meant working, paying bills, and doing the dishes like *normal* people, then I didn't approve of my lifestyle either. 'Cause those things suck."

Hannah laughed so hard that she snorted. And then laughed harder. She blamed it on the wine. "I'm so sorry," she said when she finally got herself under control. "Not funny. I know. Hurtful.

I don't know why I did that. I'm not drunk. Honest. Although that would be a better excuse than me just being a jerk."

"You were laughing so hard that I think you missed the fact that I was laughing with you."

"You're right. I missed it. Apparently, it's all about me. I'm sorry."

"Stop apologizing. It's fine. As we know, I didn't become a single mother, so I don't know how my father would have dealt with that, but he did get over me being a lesbian. He can even say the word *gay* now without having a seizure."

Hannah had the urge to laugh again but held it back. "I'm glad he came around. Do you plan on telling him about Cassidy?"

"Absolutely. I would like them to meet at some point. I know Cassidy has your family and that's important. But I hope you can understand that I want my family to know her, too."

Hannah did understand, because she would have felt the same way if the roles had been reversed. "I do."

They sat once again in silence as the night closed in around them. Hannah's head cleared, letting her know it would be safe to drive. "I'm going to get going. I'm sure you still have a lot to do before you go to bed. I hope I haven't kept you from anything important."

"Not at all. I did what was important to me today."

Hannah wondered if she was referring to them spending time together. She decided she must mean taking care of the horses and her stable. Hannah rose. She took a couple of tentative steps and decided, yes, she was perfectly fine to drive.

Maggie walked Hannah to her car, and without hesitation on Hannah's part and seemingly none on Maggie's, they both went in for a hug. It lasted a few beats longer than a normal *friend* hug and Hannah wasn't sure if it was her or Maggie who was responsible for that. Neither one had pulled away, so the answer was both.

Maggie leaned in to kiss Hannah on the cheek—not that unusual for any one of Hannah's friends to do—just as Hannah turned her head to say something. Maggie missed her cheek and her lips landed squarely on Hannah's. No conscious thought went into the next few minutes—or was it hours? Hannah pressed her lips into Maggie's and pulled her body in tight. She felt Maggie respond and it urged Hannah on. Hannah was immediately wet. Hungry with desire. Out of her mind. Yes. She must be out of her mind. She pulled out of the kiss. Her lips wet. Swollen. On fire. The tingle traveled straight from her mouth to between her thighs. She needed to leave. Now.

Without another word she got in her car, started the engine, and backed up until she was on the street. She put the car in drive and drove. Touching her still sensitive lips, she wondered what the hell had just happened.

CHAPTER NINE

There had been a few times Maggie had imagined what it would be like to kiss Hannah, but she never planned on it actually happening. And what a kiss it was. She wasn't even sure which one of them had started it. But she sure as hell knew which one of them ended it.

Hannah had pulled away and ran as if she had been burned, making it very clear that she hadn't wanted that kiss. But Maggie was sure that in the moment Hannah was right there with her. What the hell?

She stood in the driveway for several minutes trying to figure out what had just happened. She didn't get any answers. She made her way down to the barn to finish the chores for the night, and found a note tacked to the barn door.

Hey boss,
I finished the chores. I'm hoping you got home late and had a great time. Go have a drink and relax. I'll see you tomorrow.
Randi

Maggie smiled. Hiring Randi had been one of the best decisions she'd ever made. She did have a great time—right up until Hannah tore out of there. She grabbed the bottle of wine and glasses on her way into the house. She poured what was left in the bottle into her glass and settled down in front of the television. The images from some eighties rerun flashed before her without them reaching her brain. Her thoughts were on the day with Hannah and that kiss. That. Kiss. She replayed it in her mind and her body reacted all over again.

She wondered for a minute if her vibrator had batteries in it, then dismissed the idea, knowing it wouldn't satisfy her. It would only make her want Hannah more. It was so fucked up. All of it. Finding out about Cassidy. Falling for the woman who raised her. Allowing a kiss that sent Hannah running. So. Fucked. Up.

She got herself ready and went to bed. But sleep eluded her. Shadows from the moon and trees outside her window danced on her ceiling making shapes that turned into things. People things. People with lips. Hannah's lips.

By the time morning brought sunshine through the same window, Maggie had probably only logged a few hours of sleep. That sleep included dreams of Hannah. How could one kiss have such an effect on her?

She skipped breakfast, pulled her hair into a ponytail, and headed out to the barn. "Hey, guy. How'd you sleep? Better than me I bet," she said to Clover when she got to his stall. She saddled him and led him outside.

He blinked against the bright morning sun. With her foot in the stirrup, she pulled herself up and easily swung her other leg over Clover's back and eased down onto the saddle.

She started him out at a slow trot, moved him up to a canter, and then a full gallop where the trail opened up. She became one with the horse and his movements became hers. Nothing else cleared her head like the sun on her face, the wind whipping through her hair, and a horse underneath her.

Randi was heading into the barn with a wheelbarrow of fresh hay by the time Maggie returned.

"I was hoping you had Clover and he hadn't been stolen during the night."

Maggie dismounted and handed the lead to Randi. "Would you mind cooling him down, then put him in his stall so he can eat?"

"What's going on in that pretty little head of yours? You never ride this early unless there's something on your mind."

Part of the joy of having such a good friend like Randi was that she knew Maggie so well. That was also part of the problem. Maggie wasn't sure she wanted to share what had happened with Hannah the night before. She also knew that Randi wouldn't press the issue if Maggie didn't want to talk about it.

"Yeah. Stuff on my mind."

"Want to talk about it?"

Maggie shook her head. No. She wasn't ready to talk to Randi about it. But she did want to talk to Hannah about it. She just wasn't sure Hannah wanted to talk to her.

Hannah got to the flower shop early. No sense staying in bed when you couldn't sleep. What had she been thinking kissing Maggie like that? And then running. Like an asshole. She wouldn't be surprised if Maggie never wanted to see her again.

As bad as she felt about kissing Maggie she felt good about the kiss itself. It had lit up places in her that she had all but forgotten even existed. She couldn't believe how wet she had gotten from one little kiss. Okay, not little. Passionate. One passionate kiss. A kiss she wanted to repeat. Again and again. But if that one kiss was a stupid mistake, more would just compound the stupidity.

Maggie had responded to that kiss. What did that mean? *God. One kiss and I can't get it out of my mind.*

Hannah retrieved a box from the storage room in the back and pulled out six glass vases. She lined them up on the worktable and laid several bunches of various flowers next to them and proceeded to add water, snip stems, and arrange the flowers in the vases. Trying to concentrate on work was the only thing that Hannah figured would get Maggie out of her head.

It worked for a little while and then her thoughts would stray back to her. That was how most of her day went. Make a flower arrangement—think about Maggie. Wait on customers—think about Maggie. Order supplies—think about Maggie.

Cassidy was already home when Hannah walked through the door, legs pulled up underneath her on the couch, phone in her hand. Probably looking at Facebook or playing a game.

"How was your day, Mom?" she asked without looking up.

What a difference a few years made. Cassidy went through the typical teen years, not taking much interest in Hannah and pushing Hannah's rule and her patience as far as she could get away with. This Cassidy was so much easier to live with.

"Good. How about you?"

"Same. Gabby is coming over in a little while. I thought we could order a pizza."

The idea of not having to make dinner appealed to Hannah. "Sure."

"Don't forget you said you would go with me to Maggie's tomorrow. Did you make sure Becca can cover the shop?"

Shit. Hannah had forgotten about that. She would just have to plaster a smile on her face and pretend nothing had happened. "I set it up with Becca a few days ago. I'll text her to make sure she remembers."

"Thanks, Mom."

"Sure, kiddo."

Smile. Pretend nothing happened. No problem. It was her feelings that were the problem. It was getting harder and harder to pretend they didn't exist.

❖

"I'm so glad to see you—both." Maggie gave Cassidy a quick hug. It was obvious that Hannah wasn't much in a hugging mood. She quietly slipped by them and kept her distance from Maggie. Maggie chose to ignore it and act like everything was normal. Normal. There was nothing normal about any of this.

"You too," Cassidy said, although Maggie wasn't sure she meant it.

"Let's go sit outside, if that's okay with everyone. It's too nice a day to spend it cooped up in here."

"Sure," Cassidy said.

Hannah nodded.

Maggie brought out a tray of munchies and drinks and set it on the patio table on the deck. She cranked the handle on the umbrella to give them some shade. "Help yourselves." She waved a hand at the food.

"Cassidy, how is work going?"

"Good. I really like working with the kids. And you know how I feel about horses."

Maggie smiled. "Yes, I do. And I totally understand. We can go for a ride in a little while if you want."

"That would be great."

"Are you all right with that, Hannah? I don't want you to feel deserted," Maggie said.

"I'll be fine," Hannah answered.

Maggie was glad to see that Cassidy helped herself to some of the snacks. She chalked it up to Cassidy feeling more comfortable here than she did on their first visit.

"I was wondering about my father," Cassidy said between bites.

Hannah knew sooner or later she would be asking about him. Her curiosity about her inherited traits was what got them here in the first place.

"He wasn't someone that I knew. I used a sperm donor. I can go get his information, if you want. It's in the filing cabinet in my office."

"Yes. Please."

"Sure. Be right back." Maggie slipped through the sliding glass doors and disappeared into the house.

Hannah took the opportunity to check in with Cassidy. "How are you doing?"

"I'm all right. Maggie's nice. It seems a little less weird to be here than it did the first time. But, to be honest it's still kind of..." Cassidy paused. "I don't know. It's—"

"It's hard to put into words, isn't it?"

"Yeah. It's like watching a sci-fi movie that I have a starring role in. Like suddenly I'm in an alternate reality."

"I get it."

Maggie reappeared with a folder in hand. She thumbed through the contents and pulled out a single piece of paper. "Here ya go." She handed the sheet to Cassidy.

Cassidy took in an audible breath and read the information out loud.

"Hair color, light blond. Eyes, green. Fair complexion."

As much as Cassidy wanted to know about her biological father, Hannah knew it was hard for her, because she also had a biological mother now to get to know.

"Above average intelligence." Cassidy paused and looked up at Hannah. "So that's why I'm so smart."

Hannah smiled. "I always figured you took after me," she said. Her smile faded as she realized that Cassidy didn't get anything from her. Nothing. She got her looks from Maggie, her love of horses too, and her intelligence from both biological parents.

Maggie seemed to notice Hannah's emotional shift. "She got so much from you, Hannah. Eighteen years of love, kissing boo-boos, fixing scraped knees, reading bedtime stories. You have raised a beautiful, kind, loving, human being. You have a lot to be proud of."

Hannah appreciated Maggie's attempt to make her feel better. It did help. A little. "Go on, Cassidy. What else does it say?"

Cassidy continued. "Athletic, no. Ancestry listed as European, but nothing specific."

Hannah's interest was piqued. It all sounded very familiar. "Is there a donor number on there? It should be at the top."

Maggie looked at her and raised her eyebrows.

"Um, twenty-seven thirty-two. Why?"

"No," Maggie said, obviously thinking what Hannah was thinking.

"Yep. It's the same donor we used. I wonder how much that factored into the mix-up," Hannah said.

Cassidy's eyes got wide. "Wow." She looked down at the paper in her hand again and then at Maggie. "How come you chose this guy? I know my mom did because he kind of matched Mama Teri."

"Well." Maggie seemed to think about it for a few moments. "He was intelligent. I've always liked blonds, not that dark hair isn't nice too. If you read down a little more under hobbies was horseback riding, fishing and, if memory serves, camping. He sounded like a real outdoors type of person."

"We kind of just went off the physical characteristics and intelligence," Hannah said. "He was the closest match to Teri that we could find. I don't even remember reading about his hobbies, although we must have."

"Are you guys going to go back to the fertility place and find out what happened?" Cassidy asked.

Hannah looked at Maggie and realized that it was the first time since they arrived that she made eye contact with her. She was embarrassed by that. They weren't kids. She could act like an adult. "Yes. At some point we will. We don't want this to happen to anyone else." She pulled her attention away from Maggie and looked at Cassidy. "What do you think about that?"

"I think you should. They really fucked up." Cassidy covered her mouth. It wasn't the first time Hannah had heard her swear. It probably wasn't the thousandth time. But she didn't usually swear in front of other adults.

"You're right," Maggie said. "They fucked up. But you are the result of their error. And you, my dear, are not a mistake."

Hannah could tell Cassidy was touched.

"Maggie's absolutely right, honey," Hannah said. "I wouldn't trade you for the world. I'm not sorry that I had you."

"Thanks," Cassidy said, addressing them both.

"What else do you want to know, Cassidy? That's all the information I have on the donor. I'm assuming you don't have any other info on him, do you, Hannah?"

Hannah shook her head. "No. I had the same information sheet."

"What nationality are you?" Cassidy asked Maggie.

"I'm a quarter Italian, a quarter Greek, and some French in there somewhere."

"That would explain my DNA results," Cassidy said. She asked some questions about Maggie's family and Maggie filled her in on the details.

"So, I have two cousins?" Cassidy asked.

"You do. Riley is a year older than you and Jenna is three years older," Maggie said.

"Do they know about me?"

"Not yet. I told Jean—I guess that would be Aunt Jean to you." Maggie seemed to rethink her statement. "Not that you have to call her that if you don't want to. Anyway, I told Jean. She hasn't told the girls yet. I asked her not to tell anyone until I had a chance to get to know you."

"Only Jean knows?"

"So far. Yes. I would like my family to have the chance to meet you when you are ready. Do you think that would be okay?"

Cassidy shrugged. "I guess."

"There's no rush."

Hannah was thankful Maggie wasn't pressuring her.

The conversation turned much more superficial after that, and Cassidy seemed more relaxed with the change in direction.

"How about that ride now?" Maggie asked.

Cassidy's face lit up.

"You sure you're okay?" she asked Hannah.

"I'm fine. You two go. Enjoy." She watched them make their way down to the barn and come back out several minutes later with two horses in tow. She watched in amazement as they both mounted their horses almost in unison in one smooth movement. She wished she could do that. Even using the mounting block to get onto Milkshake she felt clumsy and probably looked just as stupid.

She wanted to continue her lessons with Maggie but had no idea if Maggie would still want that after what Hannah did. Kissing her was bad enough, but running away like a coward was unforgivable. She hoped Maggie could find it in her heart to forgive her anyway.

She was still deep in her thoughts when her sister's ringtone played, much too loudly, on her phone.

"Hey, Sarah."

"Hi there. What are you doing?"

"I am sitting by myself at Maggie's."

"What? Why?"

"Maggie wanted to see Cassidy, and Cassidy wanted me to come along. They are off riding horses." Hannah reached for a handful of potato chips and popped one in her mouth.

"Isn't it awkward for you? Being there?"

"It wasn't before. Today. Yeah. A little."

"Why today?"

Hannah hesitated. She always told her sister everything. But she wasn't sure she wanted to tell her how she'd made a fool of herself.

"Hannah? Still there?"

"Yeah."

"Well?"

"I've been taking lessons from Maggie. Horse riding lessons, although I've only been on a horse once and Maggie walked him in circles."

"But you hate horses. Why are you doing that?"

Hate wasn't the right word. "It's more fear than not liking them. They are so important to Cassidy that I thought if I could get over it, I could go riding with her."

"You mean with her *and* Maggie. So, it wasn't something only Maggie did with her?"

Hannah gave it a few moments' thought. "Yeah, I guess that's part of it. The other part is I want to make Cassidy happy."

"So, Cassidy wanted you to do it?"

"Not really. She doesn't even know about the lessons. I wanted to surprise her."

"Okay, let's go back to the original question. Why are you feeling more awkward today?"

"Because I kissed Maggie." There, she said it. She braced herself for Sarah's response.

"In front of Cassidy?"

That wasn't the question she thought Sarah would ask.

"No. Of course not. I was over here for a lesson on Tuesday and Maggie won't take money for the lessons, so I took her out to dinner. We came back to her house, had some wine, and when I was leaving, I kissed her."

"For God's sake, why?"

Good question. *Because she is so attractive. Because I'm drawn to her. Because being with her does something to me. Because. I don't know.* So many answers went through Hannah's mind. "It was sort of an accident."

"How in the hell do you accidently kiss someone? Did you trip and in order to stop your fall you grabbed her lips with yours?"

Hannah laughed despite herself. She explained what happened with the intended cheek kiss that landed on her lips instead.

"Sounds more like she kissed you."

"It started that way, but I…um…sort of grabbed her and kissed her fully on the mouth. It wasn't a quick peck. It was a full-on, toe-curling kiss."

"Again. Why?"

"I like her, Sarah. I didn't want to. I didn't mean to. But I do."

"You must really *like* like her."

"I do. Tell me how to stop."

"Yeah. It doesn't work that way. What did she do when you did that?"

Hannah wiggled in her seat, afraid just the memory of it would make her wet all over again. "She kissed me back."

"So, what's the problem? She must like you too. I know it's a weird situation with her being Cassidy's bio mom and all, but why fight it?"

"There are so many reasons. I don't think she feels the same for one thing."

"Then why would she kiss you back?"

"My guess is that she just got caught up in the moment," Hannah said. "There's more."

"You didn't sleep with her, did you? Hannah?"

"No. I ran."

"You don't run. You don't ride horses and you don't run. Who are you?"

"I didn't actually run. I stopped the kiss and got into my car and drove away without saying anything."

"You didn't."

Hannah could feel her face flush with heat. "I did."

"That was a dickwad thing to do. No wonder you feel awkward."

"I know. I'm an ass. I just didn't know what else to do."

"Did Maggie say anything about it today?"

"No. Cassidy's here. I think she has more class than to say anything in front of her."

"It was toe-curling, though?"

Hannah stood up and paced the length of the deck. "Oh yeah. I haven't had a kiss like that in…" Hannah thought about it. She'd been on dates in the past dozen years, but no kiss had affected her quite so strongly. Especially a first kiss where you are usually jockeying for position, feeling your way, and trying not to knock teeth. Not that there would ever be another kiss with Maggie. Although the thought sent a tingle to the pit of her stomach and below. "Let's just say in a hell of a long time."

"What are you going to do now?"

"Nothing. I'm going to pretend it never happened."

"And what about Maggie?"

"It's going to be hard to pretend that she doesn't exist. But I think Cassidy should start visiting her without me. She's old enough to handle it. I mean they are out there on the trail without me. I'm sure she's doing fine."

"So, no more horse riding lessons?"

Hannah didn't want to give them up, but she felt like she had no choice. Being around Maggie was dangerous. Her *feelings* for Maggie were dangerous.

"I guess not."

"You're going to throw the possibility of love away just like that?"

Love. Who the hell said anything about love? Hannah was thinking of it more like lust. Sure, she liked Maggie, and she was apparently sexually attracted to her. But love. No way. "There is no possibility of that so I'm not throwing anything away."

"Whatever you say."

Hannah wasn't in the mood to argue. She'd had enough arguments in her own head. "Are you calling for any particular reason?" she asked.

"I didn't think I needed a reason to call my sister."

Hannah stopped her pacing long enough to rub her temples. "You don't. I'm sorry." But she wasn't sure what she was apologizing for.

"How are you doing otherwise?"

Was there an *otherwise*? It seemed like her life now revolved around the fact that Maggie was in their lives and that she was Cassidy's biological mother. And throw a kiss in to mess it up even more. "I'm okay. I think I'm just overtired. Not sleeping too good these days." She walked back to the table and sat.

"I'm sure. I'll let you go. I'm here for you anytime you want to talk."

Hannah knew that about her sister. She was always available if Hannah needed her, and for that Hannah was grateful. "Thank you."

"Love you."

"Love you, too. Bye." Against her will, Hannah's brain turned Sarah's words over in her mind. Was she throwing away the possibility of something with Maggie? No, that was just stupid. Besides, there was Cassidy to consider. Hannah was sure she wouldn't be open to the idea, even if Maggie was interested in her.

You shouldn't base your love life on your daughter's wants, the other side of her brain argued. "Stop," she said out loud, trying to get her mind to shut up.

"But I didn't even do anything?" Randi stepped around the side of the deck.

Hannah jumped. "You scared the sh—I didn't see you there."

"That's 'cause I just got here. Didn't mean to startle you." She looked around. "Are you on the phone? Or talking to yourself?"

"Myself," Hannah said, embarrassed.

Randi climbed the three steps up to the deck and sat across from Hannah. "I do that too sometimes. But only when I need an expert opinion." She laughed at her own joke.

"My opinions are nothing but crap lately."

Randi poured herself a glass of iced tea from the pitcher on the table. "That doesn't sound good. Bet you got a lot on your mind with all that's happened in the last couple of weeks."

"That's an understatement." Hannah was glad to have company and someone to take her mind off her stupid brain's opinions while she waited for Cassidy.

"Maggie too. She's been…" Randi paused. "Let's just say it was a shock for her too. She went riding yesterday morning, very early. She only does that when—" Randi stopped. "Never mind. None of my business. Forget I said anything."

So that kiss had upset her more than Hannah had realized. Or maybe it was the way Hannah drove off without saying anything. Any way you looked at it, Hannah figured she owed Maggie an apology. It was the right thing to do.

They made small talk until Randi announced she had work to do in the barn and made her exit.

Hannah was once again alone with her thoughts. And they were relentless.

❖

As much as she didn't want their time together to end, Maggie thought maybe they should head back. It wasn't fair to Hannah to leave her by herself for so long. "This would be a good place to turn around," she said to Cassidy.

Maggie was impressed with how effortlessly Cassidy turned Jake around and had him moving in the direction of home. They had kept their conversation superficial on their ride. But Cassidy was much more talkative than she had been on their first ride. Maggie was happy for the chance to get to know her daughter bit by bit. Patience, she reminded herself.

"Have you ever competed in any horse competitions?" Maggie asked as she caught up to Cassidy.

"No. I've wanted to, but they don't teach it where I took lessons. Mom's not a fan. I wish she would get over her fear."

"I used to compete and even taught it for a while." She patted her horse's neck. "Clover here is an expert jumper."

That seemed to get Cassidy's attention. "You competed in show jumping with him?"

Maggie laughed. "No. That was a long time ago. I didn't have Clover then. But I did use him to teach jumping."

"I would love to learn."

"I would love to teach you." Maggie's heart sped up by a few beats. Yes. Something she could do with Cassidy that Cassidy actually *wanted* to do. This could be a win-win. "I'll text you tonight and we can figure out a day that works for both of us. I'm pretty sure the equipment is in the storage shed. I'll have Randi help me get it out."

"That would be so great." Cassidy seemed to sit up a little higher in the saddle. She turned to Maggie. "Can we not tell my mom about this yet? I want to surprise her once I've got it down and maybe even sign up to compete."

Maggie wasn't crazy about the idea of keeping something about Cassidy from Hannah, but then again, Hannah was keeping her riding lessons from Cassidy. "Sure. It can be our secret for now."

"Thanks." Cassidy smiled all the back to the barn.

Maggie was glad that Cassidy was happy, but she still wasn't sure keeping it a secret from Hannah was the best idea.

CHAPTER TEN

T hat stuff only happens in the movies." Maggie's dad tossed the beer cap in the trash can in the corner of his small kitchen, handed the bottle to Maggie, and opened another bottle for himself.

"Yeah. Well, not this time. Her name is Cassidy." Maggie followed him into the living room and sat on the right side of the love seat—the side she knew didn't sag.

She'd offered numerous times to buy him a new love seat, but he refused. "No sense replacing it when it still has one good side," he'd told her.

He sat in the recliner next to her. It was *his* chair, and everyone knew not to sit in it.

Maggie suspected that it was well-worn in the shape of his butt.

"How did this happen?"

"We don't know exactly. Some mix-up at the clinic we both used. We haven't talked to them, yet."

"Why not? Honey, this is serious stuff. Nothing to mess around with. They're playing with people's lives."

Maggie didn't point out that she was well aware of all that. "We will. I need to talk to Hannah about it and set up a time with her. I think we should hire a lawyer."

"That's a good idea." He took a long swig of his beer. "So, I have another granddaughter, huh? Well, I'll be damned. Tell me about her."

Maggie filled him in on any details she knew about Cassidy, including the fact that she looked like Maggie and shared her love of horses. "Are you all right with this, Dad?"

"Sure. I love Jean's girls. I'm sure I'll love Cassidy too. When do I get to meet her?"

"I'm not sure. It's important that we give her time to get used to all this before we go springing a lot of relatives on her."

"Good point. I didn't think of that."

There had been a lot to think about since this whole thing started. Cassidy's feelings. Hannah's feelings. Her feelings. Her very confusing feelings about Hannah.

Maggie hadn't been sure what to expect when she told her father, but his mild reaction surprised her. He seemed to take it all in stride. She was glad he wanted to meet Cassidy. And even more glad that he was willing to wait. He was right about one thing. She and Hannah needed to confront the fertility clinic and get some answers.

She sent Hannah a text as soon as she got home. *Can we set up a time to get together? We should talk about a few things.*

Hannah finished pouring fresh water into a large container of roses just as her phone pinged. She wiped her hands on the apron tied around her waist, pulled the phone from her pocket. and stared at the text. Oh shit. Maggie wanted to talk. Hannah was sure it was about that kiss. She had some apologizing to do. She could do that. If Maggie expected an explanation, Hannah wasn't sure she could give her one. She typed out a response, erased it, typed again, and hit send.

Hannah: *Sure. When?*

Maggie: *I'm free this evening or tomorrow evening if that works.*

Hannah figured she may as well get it over with. If she didn't do it soon, she would just ruminate on it and drive herself crazy. Crazier. They settled on six thirty that evening at a park that was about halfway between them.

She had trouble keeping her mind on her work and was glad it was a slow day. She let Becca man the shop while she attempted to do paperwork in her office. She wasn't very successful as her mind continued to play out all the possible scenarios that might take place and how she would respond.

A few minutes after six, Becca popped her head in the office door. "All locked up. Need me to do anything else before I take off?"

"Nope. All set here. I'm going to hang for a bit to work on this stuff." Hannah held up a stack of papers as if she needed to prove what she was working on.

Becca gave a half-hearted salute and left.

Hannah gathered up her papers and stacked them on the side of her desk. No sense continuing to pretend she could get anything accomplished. Out of all the problems she thought could arise when she found out about Maggie, apologizing for kissing her was not one she had ever considered.

She grabbed two bottles of water from her mini fridge and headed out. She got to the park about fifteen minutes early and found the picnic tables next to the pine trees that Maggie had mentioned without too much trouble. She'd only been there about five minutes when she saw Maggie walking toward her. Her heart rate quickened. She wasn't sure if it was because of nerves or excitement. A combination of the two was the most logical answer.

"I brought you water." Hannah handed a bottle to Maggie.

"Thanks." Maggie sat on the opposite side of the table. She set a yellow legal pad and pen in front of her.

Hannah wondered if she planned on taking notes about their conversation and her apology. If so, well, that was just a weird thing to do. No sense delaying this. She cleared her throat and started. "Maggie, I'm so sorry." The sooner everything was aired out, the sooner she could get out of here.

Maggie tilted her head and squinted but didn't respond.

Okay. She wasn't going to make this easy. "I shouldn't have done that."

"I actually wanted to talk about hiring a lawyer and contacting the fertility clinic. But since you brought it up, are you apologizing for leaving without so much as a good-bye Tuesday night? Or was that good night kiss supposed to be your way of saying good-bye?" Maggie's face was expressionless.

Hannah had no idea if she was pissed or if she was joking. "The kiss was…" Was what? A mistake? An accident? A total turn-on? All of the above?

"Was what?" Maggie wasn't going to let her off the hook with a simple *I'm sorry.*

"I didn't mean it."

"It certainly felt like you meant it. You're very good at faking it."

Hannah still couldn't read her mood. "I…I wasn't faking it. I mean, yeah, I meant it, but it was an accident."

"That doesn't make me feel too good about the whole thing. Of course, you taking off like that didn't make me feel too good either."

"I said I was sorry." Hannah didn't know what else to say.

"So, you're sorry we kissed?"

"Yes. No. I'm sorry I left like that." How could she be truly sorry for a kiss that made her feel as good at that one had.

"I'm sorry you left like that too. If you want to know the truth, I'm not sorry about the kiss. I am sorry that you thought it was an accident."

Confusion. That summed up what Hannah was feeling. "You're not sorry? About the kiss?"

Maggie had briefly considered lying. But what was the sense? It was a messed-up situation, but she liked Hannah. Liked being with her. Liked kissing her. She was sure of it. What she wasn't sure of was how Hannah felt. Time to find out. "That's what I said.

Hannah, I like you." Several beats went by. No response. "Can you share with me how you feel? Honestly."

Several more beats. "We shouldn't like each other."

Maggie shook her head. "That makes no sense. And it's not an answer."

"Cassidy."

"I'm not talking about Cassidy. I'm talking about you." Maggie wondered if the frustration that was creeping in was worth the effort of trying to get Hannah to talk about this.

"But what would it do to Cassidy?"

"What has any of this done to Cassidy? *We* didn't do this. *We* are just trying to make the best of it."

"Did you like kissing me to try to make the best of this situation?"

Hannah was infuriating. "Oh my God, Hannah. Would you listen to me? Actually listen to me? I like you. You. In a different world, in a different time, I would have been hitting on you the first time I met you. It wouldn't have taken very long before *I* was kissing *you*. Are you getting that?" Maggie couldn't believe how honest she was being. She hadn't planned on sharing her feelings, but in the moment, it felt like the only thing she could do.

"I like you too."

There it was. Finally, the truth. But it wasn't enough. "What does that mean to you?"

Hannah took her time answering. "It means that I am attracted to you." She lowered her eyes as if her answer embarrassed her.

"Hannah, can you look at me?" Maggie was surprised by her own boldness. This was so unlike her. But this was important.

Hannah raised her eyes to Maggie's.

"We like each other. We're attracted to each other. Why is that a problem?"

"Because of Cassidy."

"Wouldn't she want you to be happy?"

"Yes. But—"

"No buts. I would like to see where this could go. I don't think it would harm Cassidy in any way. We don't have to tell her anything for now." One more secret to keep. They were piling up quick.

"What are you proposing?"

Maggie hadn't thought that far ahead. "How about a real date?" Yes, that seemed like the right direction. "I would like to take you out."

Hannah sucked it her bottom lip and Maggie thought for a minute that she was going to say no.

"Dinner and maybe a movie. Nothing crazy," Maggie added.

"Dinner and maybe a movie *is* crazy. This whole thing is crazy. But…" Hannah smiled. "I happen to need to eat and I like a good maybe movie."

Maggie smiled in return. It had been like pulling teeth, as they say, but she was glad she persisted. "Tuesday? Horse lesson in the afternoon, date in the evening?"

"Yes." Was that a blush creeping up Hannah's neck? "As long as I have time to go home and change in between."

"What was it you had said to me? Don't change. I like you just the way you are."

Hannah laughed. "I'll shower and just change my clothes then. Although you may like the smell of horse on me."

"You can smell any way you want to and it will be all right with me." Had that just happened? Had she really just asked Hannah out and Hannah said yes? How weird was this? Weird for sure. But good at the same time. Very good.

"Before I made a fool of myself you said you want to contact the fertility clinic."

"Yes. And you didn't make a fool of yourself. Well, maybe a little." She held up her hand, thumb and forefinger about a quarter-inch apart. "My thought is that we hire a lawyer to write a letter to see if we can get some answers."

"You're probably right. If we just show up there, I doubt anyone will tell us anything. Should we threaten to sue them as incentive? Not that we actually would."

"That would be something to ask the lawyer," Maggie said.

"Did you have someone in mind?"

"I have a business lawyer who handles stuff for the stable. I can ask her if you want. Unless you know someone."

Maggie took notes as they discussed the details. When they said their good-byes, Hannah initiated a hug and Maggie gave her a kiss on the cheek. It landed where she was aiming this time.

It was hard for Maggie to believe what had just happened between them. She'd planned on bringing up the kiss at some point, but not today, and she hadn't expected Hannah to bring it up either. But the result of their conversation had her floating. Maybe they were being crazy, but she didn't care. Having an official date with Hannah was something to look forward to. And she was.

"Are you ready?" Maggie asked Cassidy.

"I am. I'm super excited." Cassidy connected the strap for the helmet under her chin.

Maggie showed Cassidy how to set up a rail, not that Cassidy would be setting them up for competition. "We'll just set up one for now. No need to set up more until you get used to jumping."

"How come we have it so low?" Cassidy asked. "How can I learn to jump when it's like that?"

"That's the way we start when you're learning to jump, the rail is only a few inches off the ground. Listen up. This is important. The first few times you are going to trot the horse over the rail. Just trot. Got it?"

Cassidy nodded.

"You stand in the stirrups and lean forward *before* the rail, at the point the horse would start their jump. You're not putting your upper body weight onto the horse. Hold your body in position by your core muscles."

Maggie had Cassidy repeat what she'd just said.

Cassidy said it almost word for word.

"Do you understand everything so far?"

"Yes."

"After you're past the rail, gently sit back down and continue in a trot." Maggie explained. "We'll have you do that a few times to make sure you get the position right. Rider position is everything. When you can do that, we'll move the rail up to a foot. And I'll teach you how to go over it at that height."

They went into the barn and Maggie watched while Cassidy put the saddle on Clover. It was obvious that she knew what she was doing. Maggie helped her with the running martingale, designed to keep the horse from lifting his head too high.

They led Clover out of the barn and into the larger corral where they'd set up the rail. Maggie handed Cassidy a crop. "Have you used one of these before?" It wasn't something that was regularly used in Western riding.

"I've seen them in videos—I've watched tons of YouTube videos on jumping—but I've never used one."

Maggie explained the proper way to hold it while also holding the reins and how to use it. "Using the crop helps move the horse forward or sideways and can offer increased engagement before a jump. Remember to use it behind your leg, not on the horse's shoulder. Your instinct may be to use it in front of you, instead of behind."

"Behind my leg. Got it."

"When you compete, you would normally walk the course first with your horse, to get the best idea of how to ride it. We'll skip that for today seeing as one rail doesn't make it a course. Climb on up and we'll go over a few more things before we start actually jumping."

Cassidy did as she was told and seemed to listen intently as Maggie explained correct posture again, the ability to communicate with the horse, and other things she needed to know.

Cassidy mounted Clover and Maggie had her go through the positions she needed to use before the jump and after they were over the rail. She had her repeat them three more times, even though Cassidy did them perfectly every time.

"Clover's done this before, so he knows his part as long as you give him the correct cues. Take him around the perimeter of the corral a few times. Pay attention to his rhythm. You want to be one with the horse. Do you understand that?"

"Of course. I'm not new to horses, just to the jumping."

"Remember, if you start the jump too soon, Clover will know it. He may refuse the jump or go around the rail instead of over it. You need to ride up to the base. Don't ever attempt to start the jump too soon. Any questions?"

"No. I think I've got it. What's the worst that can happen?" She smiled.

Maggie didn't return the smile. "We both know the answer to that. Remember everything I told you. You've got your helmet, crop, safety stirrups…" She looked over at the rail they had set up. "Remember to start the jump the proper distance from the rail. Everything is ready when you are. You can start him around the ring anytime, then straight down the middle to the jump."

Cassidy started him walking around the corral, and by the third time around had him up to a trot, she followed Maggie's instructions exactly liked she'd been told.

"That is great form, Cassidy," Maggie said. "You've got the positioning just right. Take him around and go again."

It didn't take too many times before Maggie said they could raise the rail. They raised it one more time after that. Cassidy was doing great.

The first time Cassidy went over the rail at the new height, she and Clover flew over it as if they'd been doing it together for years.

She had an ear-to-ear grin as she slowed him down and brought him back to where Maggie was standing. "That was so dope."

"Dope, huh?"

"Yes. Mind-blowing. Can I go again?"

Maggie beamed with pride. "You've got the posture and rhythm down great. Go ahead again. Try to do everything the same exact way."

Cassidy did as well on her second attempt at that height as she had done on her first. They continued to work for the next hour. Maggie was sure she would be ready to try two jumps in a row the next time they had a lesson.

Cassidy walked Clover to cool him down, removed his gear, and gave him a good brushing before they let him loose in the field with the other horses.

"He's such a great horse," Cassidy said as she shoveled fried rice onto her plate. Maggie was glad she'd had the foresight to order Chinese food and have it delivered, timed perfectly with the end of their lesson for the day.

"A great horse still needs a great rider. You're picking up jumping like a pro. I'm very proud of you."

Cassidy beamed. "Thanks. And thanks for teaching me."

"Of course. I enjoyed it. Same time next Sunday or do you have another day you can come over this week?"

Cassidy looked at her phone. "Um, I can come on Wednesday. I get done with work at six. Unless that's too late for you?"

"No, that works. I'm done with my lessons by four thirty on Wednesdays. Should we make this a regular thing? Sundays and Wednesdays?"

"Yes. For sure."

"Did you tell Hannah—your mother, that you were coming here today?"

"I did," Cassidy said between bites. "But I didn't tell her about the jumping. I think she was surprised that I didn't ask her to come with me."

"I'm glad you feel comfortable enough to come on your own now."

Cassidy just smiled.

Maggie was positive that the horses made it a whole lot easier for Cassidy to be there. She was glad that they had that in common.

Cassidy asked her questions about competition jumping and Maggie was happy to answer them.

"Were you good when you competed?" Cassidy asked.

"I've got some trophies. I was pretty good, if I do say so myself. And I do."

Cassidy laughed. "Yes, you do."

"What's your mother up to today?" Maggie asked, hoping Cassidy didn't think it was a strange question.

"Dinner with Grandma and my aunts. It's a family thing they do every Sunday."

Maggie admired the fact that Hannah was family oriented. Maggie was close to her sister, but they rarely got together with the rest of the family for any events. "She doesn't mind that you aren't there?"

Cassidy shrugged.

"Is that a yes or a no?"

"She would probably rather have me there, but she's okay with it."

At least Cassidy hadn't lied about where she was going today. Keeping the jumping lessons a secret was one thing. Maggie didn't want to hide the fact that Cassidy had been there as well. That would just be wrong and start them off on the wrong foot. That was the last thing Maggie wanted to do.

CHAPTER ELEVEN

Before we start working with Milkshake today, I wanted to show you the draft of the letter my lawyer wrote. She wanted to get our okay before sending it to the clinic," Maggie said. "By the way, I'm very excited for our first official date."

"Me too." Hannah followed her into the house and into the living room. She'd only been as far as the kitchen before. There were no horse pictures on the wall, as Hannah imagined there would be, but there were several trophies of various sizes featuring a horse, and in some cases a rider, tucked away on the top shelf of a bookcase. The rest of the shelves were filled with books, of all things. Hannah took her for more of the outdoor rugged type than the sit down and read type.

There were a few books on horses. Not surprising. But there were also several books that Hannah recognized from her own collections, spiritual and self-help type books. Now, that was a surprise.

"Find any that interest you? You can borrow them if you want. I've got a bunch of lesbian romance on one of the lower shelves," Maggie said.

"Romance? You're into romance?" Another surprise.

"Why are you shocked? I am a true romantic at heart. I've always wanted to find someone that I could be with forever and throw one hell of a party on our fiftieth anniversary. Guess I'm running out of time for that. I would be close to a hundred by then, if not older." Maggie paused and seemed to rethink what she said. "Sorry. That sounded—"

"It sounded *very* romantic," Hannah interrupted her. "I like that."

Maggie smiled, obviously relieved. "Moving on to unromantic things, I printed this out for you." She retrieved a single sheet of paper from the coffee table and handed it to Hannah. "You can take it with you. It's pretty straightforward."

Hannah sat on the couch and read the letter silently. She looked up at Maggie. "Sounds so formal. So legal."

Maggie sat next to her. "That's what we want. Isn't it?"

"Yeah. For sure. I know it's the way we need to do it. It's just that the whole situation is anything but formal. It's so personal. Don't you feel that way?"

Maggie laid her hand on top of Hannah's and gave it a squeeze. The gesture went straight to Hannah's heart. "Of course, it's personal. Do you want my lawyer to change it? Put something in there about the way this has affected our lives?"

Hannah thought about it for a minute. "It probably won't make a difference. What do you think?"

"In a crazy way, good things have come out of it too. Like getting to know Cassidy—and you."

Hannah flipped her hand over and interlaced her fingers with Maggie's. "True. So, let's go with the letter as is. We want answers. Right?"

"Right. My lawyer thought it was a good idea to threaten to sue them. Thought it would be taken more seriously and get us more answers."

"Yeah. I saw that. Good idea, even if we don't follow through with that part."

They sat together for several long minutes, Hannah enjoying the feeling of closeness with Maggie's hand in hers. Hoping Maggie felt the same.

"As much as I like this," Maggie said. "We should get going. I'm going to teach you how to saddle Milkshake today." She stood, pulling Hannah up with her.

They made their way down to the barn still holding hands.

"The pad goes first. It helps to make it more comfortable to have a saddle on," Maggie said. She talked Hannah through each step of the way, helping her lift the saddle to put it on. She showed her how to tighten the cinch and check to make sure the saddle was snug.

Once Milkshake was ready, Maggie handed the lead to Hannah. "Walk her out of the barn."

"I've never done that before. How do I do it?"

"I know you haven't. You lead by walking in front of the horse on the left side, the same side you mount. Sometimes you need to give a slight tug to let the horse know you want him to move forward. Milkshake will follow you. Stop when you get to the mount by the fence. I'll be right behind you."

It sounded easy enough, but Hannah's fear kept her in place.

"Hannah?"

"I'm not sure I can do this." She turned and looked at Maggie.

"Do you trust me?"

Hannah nodded. She'd taken care of her so far. No reason to think she would ask her to do something dangerous now.

"It's as simple as holding the lead and walking. He isn't going to resist you. I promise you are safe."

Hannah took a couple of steps. Milkshake stayed in the same place.

"Keep walking. As soon as you take up the slack, he'll go."

Hannah began to walk, and as promised, Milkshake walked with her. She stopped right where Maggie told her to.

"See. You did great."

Hannah laughed. "Yeah. I know how to walk, but it isn't usually this frightening."

"Why are you so afraid of horses?"

"I have no idea."

"You seem fearless. You raised a daughter by yourself. That couldn't have been easy. I doubt there's anything you can't do if you set your mind to it."

"I have to say there were times when Cassidy was growing up that I wasn't sure I could do it, especially her early teenage years. I thought for sure she would be the death of me. But I'll tell you that I would kill for that kid."

"Let's hope it never comes to that," Maggie said. She went around the front of the horse and took the lead from Hannah. "We're going to start with the basics. Squat down like this." Maggie demonstrated for a few seconds and then stood up.

Hannah repeated the pose.

"The object is to have a straight line. Ear, shoulder, hip, and heel." She gently pushed Hannah's shoulder back. "All in a straight line." She placed a hand on Hannah's hip.

A surge of electricity when through Hannah at the contact. Oh my God. *It's my hip. If my body reacts like this from her touching my hip, I will probably implode if she touched me some place intimate.*

"Are you listening to me?"

Hannah pulled herself out of her thoughts. "Of course, I am. What did you say?"

Maggie shook her head. "This is important."

Hannah stood up. "I'm sorry. Lost in my head for a moment. I won't let it happen again."

"You don't want to lean forward in the saddle, or back. Everything you need to do to communicate with the horse will come from this position."

Hannah squatted again, paying attention, making sure her body parts lined up correctly.

"Good. Like that. Go ahead and stand up. Let's have you sit up on Milkshake, like we did last time."

"Are you going to walk him around again?"

Maggie shook her head. "Nope. You are going to ride him."

"Alone?"

"You got this. I think you're ready."

"You think?"

"I know. I think. I think I know."

"You are not helping here."

"I'm kidding. I wouldn't ask you to do it if I didn't think you could handle it. I'll talk you through everything. You won't be doing it alone. I promise."

Hannah paid close attention to everything Maggie told her. There was a lot more to it than Hannah had imagined. She worried that she would forget something important and not be able to turn or stop the horse.

To her amazement, Milkshake started walking when he was supposed to.

Maggie walked next to them giving Hannah instructions. "To move the horse forward, squeeze both legs slightly. When you turn, remember you're using your left leg to move the horse to the right, and don't *just* use your leg. Pull slightly back with the opposite rein, right turn, press your left calf against the horse and pull on the right rein."

Hannah followed Maggie's directions and the horse turned right. "Oh wow. He did it."

"*You* did it," Maggie reminded her.

They made several slow circles around the corral. Milkshake stopped when Hannah pulled on the reins.

"Was that so bad?" Maggie asked.

"No. I hate to admit it, but it was actually fun. Not sure I ever want to go faster than that, though."

"Oh, you'll go faster, and you *will* love it. Let's have you dismount and walk him around the ring a couple of times. That helps to cool him down, not that he had too much of a workout today. But it's good for you to get used to doing it. Then I'm going to have you help me take off his saddle and brush him."

They finished in the barn and walked back up the driveway. "I guess I'll see you again in a couple of hours. Thanks so much for the lesson," Hannah said.

"I wish you would let me pick you up instead of you driving all the way back here."

"I know, but I don't know if Cassidy will be home. It's better this way." Hannah wanted to see where it went with Maggie before telling Cassidy. If it didn't work out, she wouldn't have to tell her anything.

"Right. Okay. I'll see you soon." She leaned in for a hug.

Hannah gave her an extra squeeze before letting go.

Cassidy wasn't home when Hannah got there. She took a quick shower, blow-dried her hair, and shimmied into her little black dress. Okay, it was actually red, but her sister Sarah told her she looked good in it and that red was the new black. Whatever that meant. She was thankful for the wedding she'd bought the dress for two years ago.

She didn't always wear makeup but thought a first date—with Maggie—called for mascara, blush, and a little lipstick. First date. When was the last time she'd gone out on a date? It must have been two years at least. She'd tried the dating sites for a while, but no one she met sparked enough interest for a second date. And some of those women were downright crazy.

But this was different. She wasn't going out with someone she didn't know. She was going out with Maggie. She still found it hard to believe that the woman who walked into their lives to shake up their neat little world would turn out to be someone Hannah would be interested in. But she was. And she really wanted to see where they could take this.

One last look in the mirror and she was out the door on her way back to Maggie's. She was grateful that Cassidy still wasn't home when she left. She didn't want to have to explain why she was dressed up, and she didn't believe in lying. She would have had to figure out a way to dance around the question without really answering it.

Maggie opened the door before Hannah had a chance to knock. "Wow. You look amazing," she said to Hannah.

"Right back at you. I love that shirt."

"Thanks. I thought the evening called for something a little dressier than my normal denim." Maggie sported a pair of gray slacks and a light blue surplice top that tied at the waist showing off her bustline. The short sleeves gathered gently at the shoulders and the whole thing fell in flowy pleats. A gold chain around her neck and matching hoop earrings completed the look.

❖

"This is a really nice place," Hannah said as they walked into the restaurant.

Maggie wanted their first date to be special. "I've heard good things about it."

Maggie had made reservations and they didn't have to wait long to be seated, or to order their food.

"I'm so glad we're doing this," Maggie said.

"Me too. If you would have told me a couple of months ago that I would be sitting here with you and everything that has happened, I would have thought it was crazy."

The waiter arrived with their wine and presented it to Maggie, label first. "Madam, your 2012 Wolf Blass Gray Label Cabernet." He poured a little in her glass.

She sniffed and sipped, like she'd seen in the movies, before nodding her approval. She was no wine expert but had called the restaurant ahead of time to get advice on ordering a good bottle.

The waiter filled their glasses and left the bottle on the table.

Hannah took a sip. "I'm impressed," she said.

Maggie briefly considered letting Hannah think she knew more than she did but decided against it. "I cheated and had help picking it out."

Hannah laughed. "How does one go about cheating with wine?"

"Some guy named Burt suggested it."

"Like some random guy on the street?"

Maggie laughed and explained how she'd called ahead of time.

"Then I am impressed with your ingenuity and your thoughtfulness." She held up her glass. "To us."

Maggie gently clinked her glass against Hannah's. "I'll drink to that."

Their food arrived in short order and was as good as the wine.

"How did you come to own a floral shop?" Maggie asked between bites.

"I started it with Teri—" Hannah looked up. "Um, twenty-one years ago. I've always loved flowers. The people that come in always have a story. They may be shopping for a sweetheart, an anniversary, Mother's Day. My favorite is putting arrangements together for a wedding."

It was obvious by the excitement in Hannah's voice that after all these years, she still loved it. "That's great. And it's okay for you to talk about Teri. She was a very important part of your life."

"Thank you. I appreciate that."

"How did the two of you meet?" Maggie truly wanted to know about the woman who had captured Hannah's heart so many years ago.

"Online," Hannah said.

"You're kidding. I've never heard of any of those dating sites actually working. All I've ever heard are horror stories."

"Oh, I've got plenty of those too. I tried the sites a few years after losing Teri. Some of the women were nice, but there was just no spark. Do you know what I mean?"

Maggie did.

"And some were downright crazy. There were a few that talked and talked and talked. By the time I left I knew all about them, their ex, their jobs, their friends. You name it and they talked about it."

"And they never asked about you?"

"Oh, every once in a while they would take a breath and ask a question. But by then I didn't want them to know anything about me. I was sorry I had even told them my name."

Maggie laughed. "But it wasn't that way with Teri? Did you hit it off right away?"

"We didn't meet on a dating site. I'm not even sure they had them then. It was in a discussion group for flowers. We chatted in the group and then privately for months before actually meeting in person. And yes, we hit it off right from the start."

"She must have been a special person."

Hannah nodded. "She was. If I didn't have Cassidy when I lost her, I'm not sure I would have gotten through it."

Maggie put her hand on Hannah's. Not only to comfort her, but she felt the need to connect to her physically in that moment. "Then I'm glad you had Cassidy."

"I'm starting to feel like one of those crazy ladies that does all the talking."

Maggie smiled. "Not at all. I want to know these things about your life."

"What else do you want to know? I'm an open book, although some of my pages are a little worn and dog-eared."

"There is nothing about you that is dog-eared," Maggie said. "What was your childhood like? You have two sisters. Were you close?"

"Not so much growing up. I was the middle kid. I didn't make waves and didn't get much attention because of it. My older sister, Sarah, and I are close now. Linda, not so much." She sipped her wine. "It's not that we don't get along or love each other. I don't know. We just don't seem to have a lot in common."

"Does she have kids?"

"Yes. Two. Totally different parenting style, so we don't even have that in common. But it's okay."

"And your parents?" Maggie hoped she wasn't getting too personal with the questions, but she was truly interested.

"Sarah was a rebel growing up. Not so much now. And Linda was the baby. They took a lot of my parents' attention. Don't get me wrong. They loved me. I just didn't demand much from them. My dad died a few years ago."

"I'm sorry."

"Yeah. We all kind of rallied around my mom. We're there when she needs us—and every Sunday for dinner."

"That's so great."

"Your turn. How did you come to own your own stable? That seems to be quite the undertaking," Hannah said.

"I've always loved horses. Started riding when I was very young. I think my dad started me with the lessons to give me something to think about besides my mother." Maggie didn't want to come off as the poor abandoned child. Talking too much about her mother might make her seem that way. "Anyway," she continued. "When I was in my mid-twenties, I scrimped and saved every penny until I could afford a place. Back then it had a very small barn and I started out with just one horse. I offered lessons, and to my amazement my schedule filled up and I was able to slowly expand to what I have now."

"And you still love it." It was more of a statement than a question.

"I do." Maggie sipped her wine. She felt it warm its way down but knew not all of the heat she was feeling was from the alcohol.

"You were raised by your dad, you said?"

"Yes. He did the best he could. Thank God I had Jean. My sister is seven years older than I am and watched out for me."

"And your father never remarried?"

"No. I think he was too hurt to even consider it. And you? Never considered remarrying after Teri?"

"I dated here and there, like I said. Cassidy and the floral shop kept me pretty busy. It wasn't that I didn't have any relationships. It's just that none of them ever got that far."

"I can understand that. It was sort of the same for me. Sometimes I wonder how much my mom leaving has played into that."

"How so?"

"When I was younger and dating, I expected anyone that I cared for to leave me. I think it became a self-fulfilling prophecy. I acted like they would leave and tried to steel myself against it. I think it ended up driving them away."

"And now?"

"Now? Now I think I'm worth staying for. I like myself. I've come to realize that my mother didn't leave because of anything I did. It was her deficiency, her lack of character. Not mine."

Hannah reached across the small table and dabbed her napkin on Maggie's upper lip. "You had a little schmutz there."

Maggie found the movement super sexy. "Thanks," she managed to squeak out.

"I'm so sorry. I didn't mean to interrupt you. Please go on."

Maggie couldn't remember for a moment what she had been talking about.

"You don't lack character," Hannah said, reminding her where she'd left off. "That's for sure. And you should like yourself, because I think you're wonderful." A blush crept up Hannah's neck. "Sorry."

"You're sorry for thinking I'm wonderful?"

The blush deepened. "I'm sorry if that sounds like I'm gushing. I've had women tell me that I'm awesome on the first date, when they don't even know me. It sounded desperate to me. Yes. I'm awesome, but someone can't possibly know that about me on the first date." She smiled.

"You seem anything but desperate to me, and this may be our first official date, but it's not like we're strangers."

Hannah's smile widened. "Good point. I do know you well enough to think you're wonderful."

Maggie rested her hand on her chin. "Tell me more." She returned Hannah's smile.

Hannah shook her head. "Oh no. That's the only compliment you are getting from me tonight. Unless you kiss me, and I'm forced to tell you what a good kisser you are."

It was Maggie's turn to blush, and she could feel the heat in her cheeks.

"Damn. I'm saying all kinds of stuff I shouldn't be saying."

"Damn. You're saying all kinds of stuff that is stroking my ego."

"Does your ego need stroking?" Hannah asked.

"It never hurts."

Hannah seemed to turn serious for a moment. "Have you been hurt a lot in your life?"

The simple answer was yes. "Enough."

"No one is hurt enough. No wait. That didn't come out right."

Maggie laughed and poured more wine into Hannah's glass. "Maybe more alcohol will help you clarify."

Hannah took a sip. "Nope. Don't know how to clarify that. But I think you know what I mean."

The waiter appeared. "All set with these?" He nodded at their empty plates.

"We are," Maggie said.

"Can I interest you in dessert?"

Maggie glanced at Hannah and nodded.

He handed them each a menu and cleared their table, balancing empty plates and bowls expertly on his arm. "I'll give you a few minutes to decide," he said and was gone.

"What were we talking about?" Maggie asked.

"Damned if I know," Hannah answered.

"Oh, you were going to clarify how much hurt was enough, or something like that."

"Yeah. No. I don't think that was it. Um. We talked about your family, my family, how wonderful you are. Kissing. I think that's it. We've run out of things to talk about."

"Then there is no sense ordering dessert." Maggie set her menu on the table. "We may as well go home."

"No. Wait. I'll think of something."

"You're very funny."

"Did you decide on dessert and how did you get to the point where you liked yourself?"

"Cheesecake and it was a long process."

"Do you want your own piece of cheesecake or can we share? I'm not sure I have room for a whole piece, and I would love to hear about the process if you care to share that too."

"Wow. How did you get all those words out without taking a breath?"

Hannah shrugged. "Just talented I guess."

"Yes, we can share. I learned to share in kindergarten. Learning to like myself took a little longer. Therapy helped. But no one can tell you that you're worthy of love or anything else. You have got to come to that on your own. Some of it came with age. I think some of it is because of my horses."

"How do horses help with that?"

"Animals, especially horses, can sense your intentions, your goodness..." She paused to gather her thoughts. "Or your *not* so goodness. My horses think I'm an okay person, if that makes sense." Maggie wasn't sure she was explaining it right. She knew what she meant, but putting it into words wasn't so easy.

Hannah nodded.

Maggie hoped that meant she was getting it. "So, if they believed in my goodness, I figured I should too."

Hannah ran a single finger over the back of Maggie's hand, sending chills down her back and a warmth between her legs.

"That's very deep. And very insightful. I like that answer."

Maggie liked that Hannah understood it and she liked Hannah touching her. Liked it a lot.

"Have you decided on dessert?" the waiter interrupted them.

Maggie looked up at him. "One piece of cheesecake and two spoons, please." She gathered both menus and handed them to him.

He returned in short order, placed a spoon in front of each of them, and the cheesecake in the center of the table.

Maggie watched as Hannah scooped up a spoonful and brought it to her mouth. She flashed back to having that mouth on hers. The softness of her lips. The faint taste of wine. She squirmed a little in her chair trying to relieve the pressure that was building inside her.

"What?" Hannah asked. "You're staring."

Maggie brought her eyes from Hannah's lips up to her bright blue eyes. Beautiful blue eyes. "I'm sorry. I was just thinking."

"About?"

"Kissing you." She could see Hannah visibly swallow. "Are you okay with that?"

"With you kissing me? Or with you thinking about it?"

"Yes."

"Okay then. How about we finish this cheesecake—which is delicious by the way—and then we can go somewhere and I'll let you kiss me?"

Maggie didn't answer. Without breaking eye contact, she scooped up a large chunk of the cheesecake and put it in her mouth, chewed, and swallowed. Then another. She pointed to what was left and then to Hannah and made an eating motion.

"You want me to hurry up and eat the rest?"

Maggie nodded. "Waiter." She waved him over. "Check, please."

Hannah laughed. "Guess I better hurry." She finished the cheesecake in two bites.

Maggie paid the bill, ignoring Hannah's objections. "I asked you out. I want to pay." She left a generous tip, and they made their way out of the restaurant.

The cool night air felt good on Maggie's skin but did little to dampen the fire building inside her. She followed Hannah to the passenger side of her car, turned her around, and pinned her against it. "I want to kiss you now."

"Then what are you waiting for?"

"Permission."

Hannah reached up and placed a hand on each side of Maggie's face and kissed her gently on the lips. "Permission granted."

That was all the incentive Maggie needed to dive in, lips first. She kissed Hannah passionately and when Hannah's lips parted, she took that as an invitation to go even deeper. She slipped her tongue into Hannah's mouth and tasted her sweetness.

The moan Hannah let loose sent a surge of moisture into Maggie's underwear. She'd never gotten this wet from a kiss. Never.

She ran her hands through Hannah's hair and swept them down her back, pulling her in closer. Hannah leaned into her, slipping her leg between Maggie's thighs. Maggie pulled her mouth away and sucked in a breath.

"You like?" Hannah whispered.

"Oh shit. Too much. I like it too much."

"Is there such a thing as too much? Or is it too soon?"

As much as Maggie wanted Hannah—and she did want her—she didn't want to rush anything. This wasn't a one-night stand. This was someone she truly wanted to take the time to get to know. "Yep," she managed to squeak out. "If we don't slow down, I'm not going to want to stop."

"I'm sorry," Hannah said.

"Oh no. No. No. Don't be sorry. You are incredibly sexy, and I like it. I just don't want to do anything too soon that you may regret."

Hannah withdrew her leg. Maggie sucked in a breath.

"You're right. We need to take this slow."

"But not too slow." Maggie kissed Hannah softly on the lips. She pulled Hannah to her and away from the car, reached around, and opened the door.

"I enjoyed today," Hannah said on the ride back to Maggie's house.

Maggie gave her knee a squeeze. "Me too."

"Come in for a night cap?" Maggie asked as she pulled into her driveway.

More alcohol wasn't a good idea. Especially if she was with Maggie. Slow. It was the best idea. "I would love to, but I better be getting home. Are you free Friday evening?"

"I do believe I am. What did you have in mind?"

"I don't know yet, but if you're open to spending more time with me, I'll figure something out," Hannah said.

Maggie tapped her chin. "Hmm. Yes, I think I would be open to spending more time with you. And then more time after that."

Hannah leaned over and slipped a hand behind Maggie's head. "That's good to hear." She pulled Maggie to her and kissed her. Hard. She had trouble catching her breath when they came up for air. "I should get going."

"You should," Maggie said and pulled her in for another kiss.

It was another fifteen minutes before Hannah was in her car heading home. She was glad Maggie agreed to another date so soon. She wasn't sure yet what they would do, but she was sure she could figure out something they would both enjoy.

CHAPTER TWELVE

Y ou what?" Sarah asked Hannah.

"Went out on a date with Maggie." Hannah pulled off her sandals and slipped her feet into the water. It was cooler than she expected it to be for July. It felt good. Having a sister with a built-in swimming pool had its perks.

"Cassidy's Maggie?"

"It sounds weird when you say it that way."

Sarah slipped into the water, took a couple of steps into the shallow end, and turned to face Hannah. "But is that who we're talking about?"

"It is."

"Then I hate to be the one to tell you this, but it *is* weird."

"That's what I thought at first. But it doesn't *feel* weird. It feels right. And you're the one who told me not to fight it."

"That's not exactly what I said, and it's still weird. What does Cassidy think about this?"

Hannah squinted against the sun. "I haven't told her. I want to see where it goes first."

"Where do you want it to go?"

Everywhere. Out to eat. On long walks. Quiet evenings bingeing TV together. Hot, sweaty sex. Lots of hot, sweaty sex. "Where does anyone want it to go when you date someone? I'd like to have a real relationship with her."

Sarah let her feet float up as she lay back in the water. "I haven't heard you say that about anyone in…" She paused. "Well, never. Not since Teri."

Hannah was envious of her sister's slim figure and flat stomach. Pregnancy took that feature away from Hannah. But Cassidy had been worth it. "I haven't wanted that with anyone until Maggie."

Sarah rolled over and doggy-paddled closer to Hannah. "Are you sure she's in it for the right reasons?"

Hannah was confused. "What do you mean?"

"Are you sure she wants what you want and she's not just using you to get closer to Cassidy."

Hannah hadn't even considered that. No. She didn't need to get closer to Hannah to get closer to Cassidy. Hannah wasn't standing in the way of them getting to know each other. "She wouldn't have any reason to do that."

"Okay. I just want you to have your eyes open. If this works out for you, then I'll be happy for you. If she ends up hurting you, I'll cut her heart out with a knife."

"Holy shit, Sarah. I have never heard you talk like that. I don't think that will be necessary."

"I just don't want anyone messing with my little sister."

"I don't think murder will be called for. She seems as into me as I am into her. Kisses don't lie."

That seemed to get Sarah's attention. "You kissed her again? On purpose this time?"

Hannah lifted her leg quickly, sending a splash of water at her sister. "God, you're nosey."

"You're the one that brought it up." She sent a wave of water back at Hannah.

"Hey. You got me all wet."

"Speaking of getting wet…"

"Oh no you didn't. We are not going there."

"I was going to say, you came over to go swimming. Didn't you expect to get wet?"

Hannah laughed and slipped into the water. Her legs had adjusted to the temperature, but the rest of her erupted in goose bumps. "Yes, we kissed again. On purpose. And oh my God, it was good."

"Yeah?" Sarah smiled.

"Oh yeah. We talked about taking it slow. But it's hard. You know? I want to dive in headfirst. I haven't felt like this in so long that I forgot how good it could feel."

"I can tell. You are glowing. And all smiles. And a little bit giddy."

Giddy. That was a good word for how she felt. She let herself slip under the water as she stepped into the deep end. She leveled her body out, swam underwater to the other side of the pool, and emerged, whipping her long hair to the side and wiping the water out of her eyes. The cool water felt good. Life felt good. And the good felt unexpected.

Hannah stretched out on the lounge chair with a towel wrapped around her shoulders. Her hair was just beginning to dry. Sarah emerged from the house with two glasses of ice water and set one down on the small table next to Hannah's chair. Sarah made herself comfortable in the other lounge chair and sipped her water.

Their comfortable quiet was interrupted by the sound of Cassidy's voice. "I'm here. Hi, Mom. Hi, Aunt Sarah."

"Hi, honey," Sarah said. "Did you bring your swimsuit?"

Cassidy let the small duffel bag she'd been carrying fall to the cement. "I did."

"How'd your day go?" Hannah wasn't sure how Cassidy felt about Sarah knowing she'd just had her first therapy appointment.

"Fine. She said I'm sane. So that was a relief."

"That is a relief," Hannah said.

"What crazy person said you were sane?" Sarah asked.

"My therapist. Mom thought it would be a good idea to talk to someone about Maggie and all this stuff that's going on." Apparently, Cassidy had no problem talking about it.

"That's because you have a very smart mother," Hannah said.

"Yeah. Maggie is pretty smart," Cassidy said.

"Whoa!" Sarah said.

"Ouch," Hannah added.

"I'm just kidding. My therapist said to try not to take things so seriously and not act like this was the end of the world. Which is what it seemed like at first."

Hannah knew Cassidy was having trouble dealing with it at first, but didn't know she'd felt that bad about it. "Do you feel better about it now?"

Cassidy thought about it for a few seconds. "Yeah. It's not all bad. Diana, that's my therapist, said that the more people that love me, the better it is for me. And that having Maggie in my life doesn't diminish my relationship with Mom."

"Sounds like it was a good session," Sarah said.

Hannah breathed a silent sigh of relief. She knew Cassidy still had a way to go, but the last thing she wanted was for her kid to suffer because of everything that had happened. She was sure her own feelings for Maggie played a part in her wanting Cassidy to accept Maggie as a part of her life.

"Did you make another appointment?" Hannah asked her.

"Yeah. It's going to take more than one meeting for me to not feel like a freak over this."

"You are not a freak," Sarah said.

"I told her the same thing," Hannah added. "But I don't think she believed me."

Cassidy pulled her phone from her pocket, typed something in, and read, "*Freak. One. A very unusual and unexpected event or situation. Two. A person, animal, or plant with an unusual physical abnormality.*"

Hannah sat up. "I'll admit that all this has been an unusual and unexpected situation, but what exactly would you consider your unusual physical abnormality to be?" She was sure she had Cassidy stumped.

"My DNA," she shot back.

Hannah shook her head and leaned back. "You may be weird, but you are not a freak. I really wish you would stop saying that."

"Whatever." Cassidy picked up her duffel bag. "I'm going to go put my bathing suit on."

"Good idea," Hannah said.

"She's really had a hard time with this, hasn't she?" Sarah said as soon as Cassidy disappeared into the house.

"She has, but she seemed much better when she returned from her visit with Maggie on Sunday."

"Why didn't you go with her?"

"She didn't ask me to. I took that as a good sign that she was getting used to the idea and being around Maggie. Maggie having horses has been a godsend for Cassidy." And in a strange way for me too, she thought. If she hadn't been taking her own horseback riding lessons, she wouldn't have had a chance to get to know Maggie. And she was so liking getting to know her even better. Just the thought of her sent a surge of electricity through her.

Maggie leaned her back against the fence and read the text from Hannah.

Hannah: *Dress casually tonight. Wear something that can get messed up without you crying about it.*

Maggie: *I rarely cry when I mess my clothes up…anymore.*

Hannah: *LOL Can't wait to see you.*

Maggie: *Ditto!*

Maggie slipped her phone back in her pocket.

"Text from Hannah?" Randi asked.

"How did you know?"

"I can tell by the smile on your face."

Was she that obvious? She did seem to be smiling a lot more these days. Two extraordinary people had entered her life and she couldn't be more thrilled about it. "Yes. We have a date tonight." She kept her attention on the teenage boy riding Jake. "Remember to sit up straighter," she called to him. "You're leaning forward again."

"Where are you going? On your date?" Randi asked.

"I don't know. Hannah planned something. Something messy, I'm guessing."

"Messy or dirty?" Randi laughed.

Maggie glanced down at her. "Now those can be two very different things, can't they? I'm hoping for a little bit of both." She knew she had that smile plastered across her face again. She couldn't seem to help it.

"Much better," she called to the boy on the horse. "Go ahead and dismount and we'll get his saddle off."

"Want me to finish up the lesson so you can get ready?" Randi asked.

"How long does it take to put on a pair of old jeans?"

"Is this like one of those 'how long does it take to screw in a light bulb' jokes?"

Maggie headed toward her student, stopped, and turned back to Randi. "You can help if you want, but let's make sure he can get the saddle off by himself this time."

They finished up the lesson and Maggie went into the house to clean up and change while Randi tended to the horses.

Hannah was right on time to pick her up. She sported a well-worn T-shirt, jeans that were ripped in the knees—fashionable with the younger crowd—and just a touch of makeup. She looked beautiful.

Maggie slipped into the passenger seat and gave her a quick kiss on the lips. "Where are we going?"

"Painting." Hannah held up a bottle of wine.

"Drunk painting?" Maggie laughed.

"Maybe. Depends how fast we drink this." She set the bottle on the floor behind her. "Ready?"

"Yep."

They made small talk as Hannah drove. It wasn't long before she pulled into the parking lot of a strip mall and parked in front of Sip and Stroke.

"What is this place?" Maggie asked. "Sounds like an adult shop."

"An adult shop?"

Maggie laughed. "You know. A sex store."

Hannah smiled. "Damn. I wish I'd thought of that. This will probably be boring in comparison. We are going to paint." She waved a hand toward the shop's sign. "That's where the stroke comes in."

"And the wine is for the sip?"

"You catch on quick."

"My daddy didn't raise no dummy."

Hannah grabbed the bottle of wine, and they made their way into the place. There were about a dozen people milling about, mostly women. Several long tables were set up toward the center of the room, each holding four small easels with a canvas on it. Various paints and brushes were set at each place. A larger easel facing the tables stood at attention in the front, with a large canvas propped up on it.

"Can I have your attention, please?" one of the few men in the group shouted above the hum of conversations. "If everyone would be kind enough to grab an apron and then take a seat, we'll get started."

Hannah slipped an apron over her head.

"Let me tie that for you," Maggie said, gently turning her around. She resisted the urge to pat her on the butt. "There ya go."

Once they were settled at a table in the back, Hannah rested a hand on Maggie's knee and Maggie slipped her fingers between Hannah's. It felt nice, comfortable, familiar. Like they'd been together for years.

"My name is Chris and I want to thank everyone for coming tonight. Wine glasses are on the table for those of you who brought your own refreshments. There is a corkscrew if you need it on the far table, along with bottles of water for those that are wineless. Either way, be sure to clean your brush in the jar of water in front of each of you. I guarantee it will ruin the taste of your wine if you wash your brush in it."

Several small chuckles arose from the crowd.

He went on to explain what they would be doing, and he introduced two women who would be wandering the room to help anyone in need.

"How are you doing?" Hannah asked when they had their paintings about halfway done.

Maggie tilted her head and examined what she had on the canvas. Her moon looked okay. But she thought her tree looked a little wonky. "All right I guess." She put her attention on Hannah's painting. "Yours looks better."

"You need more wine." Hannah poured more into each of their glasses. "The more you drink, the better your painting looks."

Maggie laughed. "Then I may need to drink the rest of the bottle." She scooped up a bit of yellow paint from her palette with her finger and swiped it across Hannah's nose.

"Hey."

"Now that is a painting I like."

Hannah leaned over and gave Maggie a kiss on the cheek, rubbing her nose against her. "I like to share," she said.

"Are we ready to work on the owl?" the instructor asked the class. "Anyone need help with their trees?"

Maggie's hand went up, but Hannah pulled it back down. "Don't change a thing. I love your tree."

"Then you can have it when I'm done."

"Yes. I want it. We can trade."

Chris painted a brown oval on one of the branches of his perfect tree. "We start with a simple shape."

By the time they were done they each had an acrylic painting with an owl sitting in a tree with a big light-yellow moon behind it.

"Did you have fun?" Hannah asked Maggie.

"I did. But I have a feeling that anything I do with you would be fun." She took Hannah's hand as they walked back to the car. Hannah opened the car door for her.

"Me too. Want to grab something to eat?" Hannah asked before starting the car.

"If you wipe that paint off your nose, I do. And make sure there isn't any paint on me, while you're at it."

Hannah licked her thumb and ran it over Maggie's cheek. "All gone." She stopped and seemed to realize what she had just done. "I'm so sorry. That's a mom thing. It was always the easiest way to get dirt off Cassidy's face if I didn't have a baby wipe handy."

The statement chipped at Maggie's heart. One more thing that Hannah got to do with Cassidy that she didn't.

Hannah must have sensed something wrong. "Talk to me."

"What?"

"I saw something go across your eyes. Tell my what you're thinking."

"You said it was a *mom thing*. I didn't get to do any of those mom things. Not that I'm blaming you," Maggie quickly added. "Sometimes it just hits me how much I missed out on."

"I'm so sorry. I shouldn't have said that."

"No. I don't want you to censor yourself. I just need you to understand how some of this feels," Maggie said.

Hannah leaned over and pulled Maggie into her arms. "Thank you for telling me. I do want to know how you're feeling, and I'll do my best to try to understand and not make it worse for you. I care about you."

"Thank you."

Hannah pulled back and looked into her eyes. "Of course. I don't want you to hurt."

"I changed my mind," Maggie said.

"About getting something to eat?"

"No. I'm still hungry. I changed my mind about the paint on your nose. I think you should keep it."

Hannah laughed. The sound of it seemed to right Maggie's world. Hannah pulled her sun visor down and looked in the mirror. "It does look good on me. I think yellow's my color." She started the car and backed out of the parking spot.

Maggie was starting to really like this silly woman sitting next to her. Really, really like her.

Chapter Thirteen

"Y ou are doing so well," Maggie said to Cassidy as she came back around on Clover. "You cleared all three rails with no problem. You were made for show jumping."

"When do you think I can actually compete?" Cassidy asked her.

"You've only had a half dozen lessons. Let's give it a few more weeks at least. You'll be in the adult amateur division because you're eighteen. So, you'll be competing with people mostly older than you. I want to make sure you're ready."

"I feel ready now."

She really was doing well, but Maggie wanted her to have a lot more lessons under her belt before she went into the ring.

"I looked it up and there is a competition next week in Saratoga."

"Yeah. No. We are going to start with a smaller competition, closer to home. There's one at the fairgrounds in three weeks. We can see if you're ready then." She paused. "But maybe we can go to the one in Saratoga so you can see what they're like."

"Yes."

"Now go again. Let's make a couple more runs."

The rest of the lesson went just as smoothly. Maggie was proud of how well Cassidy was doing.

"When are you planning on telling your mother about this?" Cassidy brushed Clover as Maggie wiped down the saddle.

"Not till after my first competition."

Maggie stopped what she was doing and gave her full attention to Cassidy. "Why? Don't you want her there?"

"I want to make sure I know what I'm doing, and I don't expect to do great the first time out. I want her to be impressed."

"Oh, honey, I'm sure she will be proud. You've worked so hard."

"I know, but I want to prove I know what I'm doing."

Maggie wasn't so sure taking Cassidy to compete without Hannah knowing about it was a good idea. "I think we should let her know before that."

"Please, Maggie. Let me do one competition first. Promise you won't tell her before that."

Maggie didn't understand the desperation in her voice. But it wasn't like she was a little kid. She was eighteen. Old enough to make her own decisions. "All right, but you need to tell her right after that. No excuses."

Cassidy seemed to visibly relax. "I will. For sure."

Maggie still wasn't happy about keeping it from Hannah, but she decided to trust Cassidy on this one. She just hoped it didn't come back to bite her in the ass.

It seemed like every date with Maggie was better than the one before, whether it was a fancy dinner or a simple walk on the canal.

"I think you'll be ready to ride Milkshake on the trail the next time."

Hannah reached for her hand. It was a beautiful day for a walk. Summers in upstate New York could be hot, add in the humidity and some days were unbearable. But temps in the low seventies made the walk by the water wonderful. The company made it perfect.

"By myself?" Hannah asked.

"I'll be right next to you on Clover."

Hannah was glad she was next to her now. The warm breeze pushed the clouds above them in and out of interesting shapes.

"Okay."

"Okay? No arguments? No telling me you're afraid?"

Hannah pulled her into a hug. They were alone on the path, but Hannah wouldn't have cared if they were surrounded by other people. "I trust you. If you say I'm ready, then I must be ready. Am I afraid? I've been afraid every step of the way. But somehow you always make it all right."

"Thank you for trusting me." Maggie kissed her gently on the lips. "By the way, I was thinking, if it's all right with you, I'd like to take Cassidy to a horse show, jumping, on Friday. It's in Saratoga."

Hannah nodded. She didn't have a problem with that.

"And afterward, if she's up for it, bring her to meet my sister and nieces. I would ask her too, of course."

"Sure. As long as it's okay with Cassidy. She has come a long way since we first found out about the mix-up. I think she's ready for it. I do appreciate you checking with me first."

"Of course." Maggie kissed her again.

Hannah pulled her in tighter and kissed her. Harder. Longer. Completely. She was trembling by the time she pulled away. She couldn't believe what Maggie could do to her. She wasn't sure how much longer she could wait until she had her fully, *body* and soul. And oh, what a body it was. It looked great with clothes on, she could only image how great it would be naked.

"Wow," Maggie said.

"Wow is right. What are you doing Saturday evening?"

"What did you have in mind?"

"I'm thinking I would like to expand on this thing we call kissing." She paused. "If you're ready. I mean, I don't want to rush you."

Maggie tilted her head. "Hmm. Expand on this thing we call kissing. I think this thing we call kissing, *is* actually kissing. And to expand on that would mean—"

"Exactly," Hannah interrupted her.

"I'm thinking that I would cancel any plans I had to expand with you. Luckily, I didn't have any other plans. So, I'm all yours—to expand."

Hannah's stomach did a little flip at the thought. Yes. They'd waited long enough. She kissed Maggie again.

The sound of a splash nearby brought Hannah's attention to their surroundings. "What was that?" Hannah asked.

"Probably a frog jumping into the water. You've never heard anything like that before?"

"Hey. I grew up in the city. Not too many frogs jumping into the water there."

They started walking down the path again, hands and fingers intertwined.

"We had a pond behind us," Maggie said. "We would catch frogs and tadpoles and put them in our little blow-up swimming pool."

Hannah pictured Maggie as a kid with a fish net scooping up pollywogs. It wasn't hard to imagine. She and Cassidy probably looked a lot alike. "I would have loved to have known you as a kid."

"You're six years younger than me. No way would I have been hanging around with you." She laughed. "If I was ten collecting tadpoles, you would have only been four."

Hannah thought about it for a minute. "I probably would have been following you around, making a pest of myself."

Maggie gave her hand a squeeze. "I'm glad you grew up, because you are anything but a pest now. And you can follow me anywhere."

"I like that. What else did you do when you were a kid?"

"Normal kid stuff, I guess. My sister and I had to grow up faster than normal because of my mother leaving. I think my sister felt the need to look after me, and we both felt the need to look after my father."

"That must have been hard."

"It kind of does something to you when your mother—the one person who is supposed to love you no matter what—leaves you. I think because of that I feel even more protective of Cassidy, if that makes sense." She looked at Hannah trying to gauge the look on her face. She couldn't quite tell what she was thinking. She went on. "I mean, I know you raised her and you *are* her mother. Truly. But I feel so…" She paused trying to find the right words. "I'm not explaining this very well."

"You're doing fine. Finish your thought."

She appreciated Hannah's patience and understanding. "Even though she hasn't been in my life for that long, I only want the best for her. I guess what I'm trying to say is that I really care about her and her well-being."

They stepped off to the side of the path to let a bicycle pass by.

"I can understand that," Hannah said.

"And I care about you," Maggie continued. "Because you're Cassidy's mother. But it's so much more than that. I care about you because you're you. Does that make sense?"

Hannah nodded. "It does, because I feel the same about you."

"Good," Maggie said. "Because it would suck to feel all these feelings alone."

"Who would have thunk it?"

"Not me. I never could have ever imagined any of this." But she was so happy it was happening. So happy. Sure, she'd had relationships in the past that started out great but soured at some point. But this felt different. Even if they didn't have Cassidy to connect them, they would be connected. There was just something there. Something she couldn't quite put into words. Something she didn't want to let go of. It had been a long time since she'd dreamed of the possibility of forever with someone, but she had dreams of it now. And it scared the hell out of her.

❖

"Hi, honey," Hannah said to Cassidy. It was unusual for Cassidy to stop in the floral shop, but always a welcomed surprise.

"Hi."

Hannah tucked some baby's breath into a vase, clipped the ends on three long-stem roses, added them, and tied a red bow around it. "Want to put this in the fridge for me?" She handed it to her and started in on another. "What are you up to? How was work?"

"Good. I was going to hang with Gabby, but she has to babysit." Cassidy toyed with the spool of ribbon on the counter.

"So, you thought you would come and hang with your old mama instead?" She finished arranging the flowers and put her hand out. Cassidy handed her the ribbon.

"You're not *that* old." Cassidy smiled.

"Geez, thanks."

"Speaking of hanging out with old people. I'm going to go to a horse show with Maggie tomorrow."

"Maggie's not old." Hannah didn't let on that Maggie had already told her about the trip and asked if it was all right with her.

Cassidy ignored her comment. "It's in Saratoga." She scrunched up her face and bit her bottom lip.

Hannah knew from that look that Cassidy expected her to object. It was a two-hour drive, but Cassidy was old enough to make her own decisions and she trusted Maggie with her—with just about everything. "Okay."

"Okay?"

"Sure. Do you want to go?"

"Of course."

Hannah handed Cassidy two more vases filled with roses and baby's breath. "Okay. Go and have a good time. Tell Maggie I said hello."

"Thanks, Mom."

"What time do you think you'll be home?" Hannah wondered if she could invite herself to Sarah's for dinner.

"Why? Do you have a hot date?" Cassidy laughed.

"Is that funny? The thought of me dating?"

"Kind of. Yeah."

It wasn't funny. Just because she hadn't dated in a while and Cassidy didn't know she was dating Maggie didn't make it funny. Hannah didn't bother replying. Instead, she walked around Cassidy and started plucking wilted petals off the flowers in the bouquets by the counter.

"You don't think it's funny?" Cassidy wasn't going to let it go.

Hannah turned to her, hand full of flower petals and looked up at her. "No. Why would I think it would be funny? Do you think I'm too old to date? Or too grotesque?"

"Chill, Mom. I'm just teasing you. You just haven't dated in so long. I didn't think you had any interest in it anymore."

"Well, I do. I'm not so old that I can't be interested in someone special." Shit. Too much. She immediately regretted her words and hoped Cassidy wouldn't ask anything else.

"Are you? Interested? In someone? Someone special?"

Yep. She asked. Hannah wasn't ready to tell her about dating Maggie yet. Yes, it was going great. Yes, she was ready to take the next step with her. But what she wasn't ready for was telling Cassidy. For a moment she wondered why. If she had been dating anyone else *besides* Maggie, she would have told Cassidy by now. Why did she hesitate? Because it was weird. And the situation itself was weird enough without throwing in the fact that Hannah was falling for the woman who was Cassidy's biological mother.

"I'm just saying I'm not too old for that." Not the whole truth, but not a lie either.

Cassidy gave her a strange look. Hannah could almost see the wheels turning in her head, trying to decide if she should dig further.

Time for a diversion. "If you were going to be late tomorrow, I thought I would see if Aunt Sarah would let me come over for dinner." There, that was the truth and hopefully would end the conversation about dating.

"Okay. Besides, I was just joking."

The bell over the door rang as it opened, and three boxes on a hand cart entered, followed by the UPS man. Perfect timing.

"Delivery. I just need a signature," he said. "Where do you want these?"

"By the side of the counter would be great." Hannah signed his electronic clip board.

"Have a nice day, ladies," he said and was gone.

"Get anything good?" Cassidy asked, tapping the bottom box with her toe.

"Supplies. Floral wire, tape, vases. Want to help me put it away?"

Cassidy let out a huff. "Sure. I live to organize."

"Good to hear. Maybe you can organize your room once in a while."

"Hey. I cleaned it last week."

"I was just joking. See. How do you like it?"

Cassidy wasn't known for her cleaning skills. What eighteen-year-old was. She had more important things to do, like horses, friends, and the occasional boy crush. Boys had been put on the back burner for the summer while Cassidy concentrated on working at the stable and hanging with Gabby. Throw Maggie into the mix and Cassidy didn't have much time for dating.

Hannah was sure that would change when she started college and had a slew of new boys—young men—to draw her attention. Maybe then she would tell Cassidy about her and Maggie. By then she would feel more secure in what they had, if they were still going strong. And Hannah certainly hoped they would be.

Chapter Fourteen

Maggie pulled out of the parking lot and headed in the direction of the highway. "What did you think?" she asked Cassidy.

"I loved it. I'm ready, Maggie. I really am. I can't wait to compete. Clover and I work so well together. That was so exciting. And you explained everything so great. I really loved the way the last rider worked her horse. And what a beautiful horse that was. And..."

"Take a breath there, Cassidy." Maggie laughed. "I'm getting the feeling you really liked it."

"Oh man. I did."

"I'm glad. I thought maybe we could stop at my sister Jean's house before I bring you home. She has been looking forward to meeting you. Her two girls will be there as well." She looked over at Cassidy to gauge her reaction. The last thing she wanted to do was force her to meet her family too soon. She still had trouble reading Cassidy's face—except when she was excited about some horse thing.

"Sure. Okay."

"You're sure? You're okay with it?"

"Uh-huh." Cassidy turned her head to look out the window.

Maggie had no choice but to take her at her word. It was close to two hours later by the time Maggie pulled into her sister's driveway.

"Hi," Jean said as she opened the door. "You must be Cassidy. I am so glad to finally meet you." She pulled her into a hug.

Cassidy didn't seem to mind. "Nice to meet you."

"Wow. You look like your mother...err...um...I mean Maggie. Sorry."

"That's okay. I guess we do look alike."

Maggie stuck her head around Cassidy. "Okay if we come in or should we just have our whole visit here in the doorway?"

Jean shook her head. "Of course. I'm so sorry. Come in. Come in. Can I get you something to drink?"

"Would it be all right if I used the bathroom? It was a long ride," Cassidy said.

"Down the hall, first door on the right," Maggie said to her. "We'll be in the kitchen."

Maggie followed Jean and sat on a stool at the island while Cassidy went to the bathroom.

"I'm sorry," Jean said for the third time. "I'm don't know why I'm so nervous."

"Stop apologizing. I'm sure Cassidy's nervous too. At least I think she is. I can't always tell what she's thinking. Unless it involves horses."

Jean leaned back against the counter. "She gets that from you, huh?"

"She does. Hannah is—was—afraid of horses."

"Was?"

Maggie lowered her voice. "I've been working with her to overcome her fear and teach her to ride."

"Why are we whispering?" Jean asked in an equally low voice.

"Because Cassidy doesn't know. Hannah wanted to surprise her." She looked in the direction of the bathroom before continuing. "She doesn't know we're dating either, so please don't say anything."

"How can I say anything when I don't know anything? What the hell? How come you didn't tell me? I mean I knew you liked her. But this? This is news."

"I guess I just wanted to keep it close to the vest for a while."

"Sounds like you kept it in your pocket, tucked away in a drawer, at the back of a closet."

Maggie shook her head. "That's a little overkill, don't you think? I'm telling you now."

"Yeah, when Cassidy is here, and I can't ask any questions."

Maggie shrugged. What else could she say? She usually told Jean everything. She wasn't exactly sure why she hadn't shared this.

Cassidy came down the hall.

"Come and sit down, honey," Jean said. "What would you like to drink?"

"Whatever you have is fine," Cassidy answered.

"She's not much into soda," Maggie offered.

"Apple juice?" Jean asked.

Cassidy nodded and sat on the stool next to Maggie.

"My girls should be here soon." Jean poured a glass of juice and set it in front of Cassidy. "Unfortunately, my husband, Darrel, has to work late, so you'll have to meet him another time. I thought maybe we could order a pizza in a little while. But would you like a snack or anything now?"

"No, thank you."

Maggie tried to gauge Cassidy's comfort level. She seemed okay but was very quiet. Of course, she had been pretty quiet the first time she met Maggie too.

"We went to a show jumping competition today," Maggie said. "Cassidy, why don't you tell Jean about it? Cassidy is taking jumping lessons from me."

Cassidy's face lit up. "It was really cool," she said and proceeded to tell Jean the highlights of the day. Jean's daughters showed up together just as Cassidy finished.

Jean did the introductions, and it didn't take long before the three girls were chatting away. Both girls were home from college for the summer. Riley was attending her second year at the local community college in the fall.

"I'll be going there too," Cassidy said. "Do you like it? What are you majoring in?"

"I do. Art, but they make you take a bunch of other stuff too," Riley answered.

"Like what?"

"English. Gym." She made a face and shook her head.

"You don't like gym?"

"Hate it. I would rather spend my day painting or drawing. My mom said you like horses, like Aunt Maggie. You can choose horseback riding instead of swimming or volleyball or whatever. So, you would probably like it."

"Want to go hang out on the back deck?" Jenna asked her. "We can listen to music."

Cassidy looked at Maggie and raised her eyebrows. Now, that expression Maggie understood. She gave Cassidy a wink. "Go have fun. Get to know each other."

They didn't need to be told twice and were out the door without another word.

Jean put up a finger, stuck her head into the dining room, returned, and sat next to Maggie.

"What did you just do?" Maggie asked her.

"I wanted to make sure they closed the patio door. Now spill. You're dating Hannah? How long has this been going on? Have you slept together? How did this happen? I mean who asked who out?"

"Oh my God. That's a whole lot of questions at once. Usually a conversation consists of someone asking a question and allowing time for the other person to answer."

"Since when are you such a stickler for protocol?"

"Since you are jumping all over me with questions," Maggie said.

"Here's a question. Do you want some wine?"

Wine would have been very welcomed, but she still needed to drive Cassidy home. She passed. "But you go ahead."

Jean poured herself a glass. Maggie took a sip as soon as she set it down.

"Hey." She got another glass and poured about half as much wine in it and handed it to Maggie. "A little's not going to impair your driving. And it will probably help to loosen your tongue. Now tell me how this whole thing started." She sat back down.

"I opened an email that said I had a new DNA relative." Maggie sipped her wine.

"Ass. I know that part. How did you and Hannah start dating? When did you start dating? Oh shit. That's more than one question."

"We kissed."

"What? You kissed? When? Before you started dating?"

"Are you going to let me answer?" Maggie pushed Jean's wine glass closer to her. "Drink and be quiet."

Jean pantomimed zipping her lips, locking it, and throwing away the key. It was something they had often done as kids. Maggie hadn't seen her do it in years.

"Gonna be hard to drink your wine with your lips zipped closed."

Jean made a rolling motion with her hand, indicating Maggie should continue.

"Yes. We kissed. We didn't plan it. It just sort of happened. And then Hannah took off." She waited for Jean to ask the next inevitable question, but she remained quiet. And very attentive.

Maggie continued. "We had been working together to help her get over her fear of horses, so it wasn't like we were total strangers. But I think it scared her. Anyway, she ended up apologizing." Maggie filled Jean in on most of the details and how she was the one to ask Hannah out.

"I have always admired how brave you are," Jean said. "I would have been peeing my pants with nerves."

"It did make me nervous. But I really like her, and judging from that kiss, she liked me too. I don't think I would have ever forgiven myself if I didn't take that chance. I figured the worst that could happen was that she said no. But she didn't." She sipped her wine. "And, Jean, it's been so good."

❖

"That is so good," Hannah said.

"You like?" Maggie asked.

"Yes. You aren't going to convince me that you aren't a wine expert."

"I am a Google expert."

Hannah finished her last sip and set her empty glass on the coffee table. One glass was perfect. Enough to relax her without sending her head spinning.

"They called that a dessert wine. I think it was the perfect way to finish our meal."

"That meal was wonderful. I had no idea you could cook like that. But to be honest I had something else in mind for dessert, besides the wine. Not that the wine wasn't appreciated."

"You had something else in mind?"

"I did. It involved you and me—expanding." Hannah had never been this bold in her life. She wanted Maggie and she didn't want to wait any longer. "What do you think?"

"What does this tell you?" Maggie pulled Hannah into her arms and kissed her. Hannah parted her lips and welcomed Maggie's velvety soft tongue in. She felt light-headed as the blood from her brain rushed to her center.

Their tongues wrestled for control and Hannah let Maggie win. It was only a matter of minutes before their clothes were shed and Hannah was on her back on the couch, Maggie's thigh pressed between her legs.

Maggie had Hannah's breast in one hand and slipped her other hand between Hannah's thighs. Hannah gasped as Maggie ran a single finger through her folds.

"You are so wet," Maggie whispered.

"That's what you do to me."

"I like what I do to you." She pressed her lips to Hannah's and plunged her tongue into her mouth, sweeping through it like a tornado.

Maggie's mouth held Hannah's moan in place, refusing to let it escape.

The weight of Maggie's well-toned body on hers increased Hannah's pleasure immeasurably. It was a sensation she never wanted to stop and at the same time she thought she might implode from the wonder of it. Every fiber of her being was on fire.

Maggie slipped off her and Hannah let out a whimper at the loss. Before she had a chance to register what was happening, Maggie was on her knees on the floor and Hannah's legs were spread apart with Maggie's face between them. Maggie's tongue was doing incredible, almost indescribable things to her.

Hannah lifted her hips off the couch with a rhythm that matched Maggie's movements.

The finger Maggie slipped into her touched places that Hannah had forgotten she had. When she added a second and then a third, Hannah was sure she would die from sheer pleasure. The pressure built to a level Hannah didn't know existed. She longed for release and at the same time tried to keep it from happening to prolong the sensations coursing through her.

As if Maggie could read her mind, she eased up, delaying her impending orgasm.

Hannah took the opportunity to breathe, releasing the breath she'd been holding. The reprieve was short-lived, and Maggie plunged her tongue deep into Hannah while she increased the pressure of her fingers.

Lights flashed behind Hannah's closed eyelids and a sound like a freight train filled her head as her hips bucked and her release came in a rush that seemed to last longer than any she could remember.

Maggie slowed her movements but kept the pressure steady until Hannah felt a second round of contractions as a second orgasm swept through her.

Hannah could taste herself on Maggie's lips when Maggie moved from between her legs to her mouth, kissing her gently. Her kisses traveled to Hannah's cheek, her neck, her shoulder, the center of her chest. She moved first to one breast, sucking in a nipple, and rolling it around her mouth with her tongue before showing the other breast the same attention. Hannah's breath caught in her throat.

Maggie's quieted fingers still inside her, her mouth on Hannah's breast—it was almost more sensation than Hannah could take. Almost.

"You're going to kill me," she managed to whisper.

Maggie removed her mouth long enough to respond. "Oh, what a way to die."

Hannah pulled Maggie's face up to hers and kissed her gently at first and then with more passion. Her body responded all over again as Maggie moved her fingers once more inside her. Her third orgasm came quick. Powerful. Mind-blowing. Hannah groaned as Maggie's fingers slipped out of her.

"That was better than anything I've imagined," Hannah said when she could catch her breath.

"You've imagined this? You and me?"

"You haven't?"

"Oh yes, I have. It's been hard to think of anything else lately."

Hannah sat up, still feeling a little shaky as her blood redistributed throughout her body. "Come up here. It's time you stop thinking about it and start letting me show you." She patted the couch next to her.

"I like it when you take charge." Maggie sat next to her.

"You ain't seen nothing yet." Hannah's mouth was on hers before she had a chance to respond. Maggie's nipple hardened under her touch. She rubbed her palm against it, squeezing Maggie's breast in her hand. It fit perfectly, as if it was made especially for Hannah. She bowed her head and sucked the other nipple into her mouth.

The deep moan that came from Maggie's throat urged her on. It hit her square in her center and she felt herself get aroused all over again. She couldn't get enough of this woman next to her.

She ran her tongue around Maggie's nipple, down her rib cage, and around her belly button. She slipped off the couch and knelt in front of Maggie. Wrapping her arms around her, she pulled her forward until Maggie's butt was close to the edge of the couch, giving Hannah access to the spot she desired.

She couldn't wait to taste Maggie but paused to take in the beauty before her. Maggie had her eyes closed and Hannah ordered her to open them and look at her. "You are so gorgeous," she said. "You have no idea how incredibly sexy you are."

Hannah watched a blush creep up from Maggie's neck to her face before Hannah lowered her head and slipped her tongue between Maggie's folds, taking in all Maggie had to offer. She positioned herself in such a way that she could have her way with Maggie's most sacred place and still see Maggie's face if she tilted her head just right.

Maggie threw her head back against the couch and squeezed her eyes closed. Her breathing became rapid and the skin on her face flushed. Hannah listened to every wonderful sound that came out of her and coordinated her movements based on them.

Hannah's own excitement was building as Maggie's body responded to her. Hannah loved the effect she had on Maggie and the effect Maggie had on her. She slipped a finger through

Maggie's folds into her wetness. Maggie sucked in a breath. Her muscles tightened around Hannah's finger as she rode the wave of her climax.

Hannah pressed her tongue hard against Maggie, flicking it as Maggie was coming down, sending her to new heights.

Maggie grabbed the back of Hannah's head, keeping her in place. Not that Hannah had any plans to pull away.

"Oh God, oh God, oh God," Maggie said in rapid succession.

Maggie gently tugged on Hannah's head, pulling her up to Maggie's face where she planted kisses on her nose, her forehead, her lips.

Hannah leaned into her, their arms wrapped around each other, their heartbeats occupying the same space. She never wanted to leave this envelope of safety and feelings.

"Come to my bedroom with me," Maggie whispered into Hannah's ear.

Hannah pulled back just enough to look into her eyes.

"I want to lie in bed next to you. Naked. And just hold you."

Hannah started to say something about needing to spend the night at home, but Maggie cut her off.

"Just for a little while. I know you have to leave soon."

"That is just about the most romantic thing anyone has ever said to me."

Maggie kissed her on the mouth. "I told you I was a romantic."

Hannah stood, took Maggie's hand and pulled her up. They made their way to the bedroom. Maggie pulled down the covers and they climbed in together. Hannah snuggled closer, wrapped her arms around Maggie, and tucked her head under Maggie's chin.

"Thank you," Maggie said.

"For what?"

"For being here. For being you. For that amazing orgasm."

"It was my pleasure. Believe me. My pleasure. This evening—with you—has been amazing. Warm. Wonderful. And I feel…" She tried to put her plethora of feelings into words. "I feel complete. Yes. That's the right word. Complete. I haven't felt like that in a very long time." She raised her head to look into Maggie's eyes. "Not that I need you to complete me." She shook her head. "This isn't coming out right." She took a few moments to get her thoughts in order. "I guess what I'm trying to say is I feel full. Content. Happy."

"Me too."

"Oh sure. I struggle for all the right words and you just jump on the bandwagon," she teased her.

"You picked all the perfect words. You didn't leave many for me. But I'll add that I adore you and I'm so glad you came into my life. You enhance my world."

"I don't complete you?"

"No, Tom Cruise, you don't complete me. But you do make me extremely happy."

CHAPTER FIFTEEN

The next couple of weeks flew by. Hannah's first horseback ride on the trail, with Maggie right beside her on Clover, went well. She felt like she had made leaps and bounds since their first lesson when she was afraid to even touch Milkshake. Maggie was a good teacher—and a fantastic lover. Hannah couldn't seem to get enough of her.

Everything was right on track for Cassidy to start her first year of college. Orientation was just around the corner. And she made sure she could take her classes and still give riding lessons to the kids.

Life was feeling pretty darn good for Hannah.

"The lawyer got a letter back from the fertility clinic," Maggie told Hannah over lunch. "It included a report on their investigation into how this happened."

Hannah set her sandwich down. "What did it say?" Her stomach suddenly tight.

"I printed it but didn't read it yet. I thought we should do that together after lunch. Finish your sandwich."

"I don't think I can eat now. I'm surprised you can," Hannah said.

"What can it tell us that could make anything worse? We've lived with this for weeks. And we've survived." She took Hannah's hand. "Thrived in fact. That report isn't going to change anything."

"You're right. It won't change anything. But hopefully it will give us answers."

"Okay. Let's go?" Maggie pushed her chair back.

"Where?"

"To get our answers. The papers are in the living room."

Hannah followed her and sat on the couch. Maggie scooped a manilla folder from the coffee table and handed it to her. Maggie remained on her feet, shifting her weight from one foot to the other.

Hannah stared at the folder in her hands for several long seconds. Whatever was in that folder wouldn't change anything. What was done was done. But she needed to know how this had happened.

She opened the folder, took the letter from the lawyer, and put it on the coffee table. She thumbed through the report. It was three pages long. Three pages to explain how she gave birth to Maggie's child. Three pages to explain how their lives had been turned upside down. Three pages didn't seem like it was nearly enough.

The first page was mostly things they already knew. Their names, doctors' names, addresses at the time of the procedures, and such.

Hannah looked up at Maggie. "We had our egg retrievals two days apart. Two from you and four from me. And we had the same doctor."

"Dr. Daniel Harris," Maggie said.

"Yes. But we had the embryos transferred the same day. Both of yours were viable. Two of mine were." She glanced at the paper again. "Your appointment was an hour after mine."

It didn't matter how much Hannah already knew. This still seemed so unreal. She continued. "Normal harvest, blah, blah, blah, embryos viable three to five days after, blah, blah, blah." She turned the page. "The findings of our investigation are as follows."

Hannah looked up at Maggie and reached for her hand. Maggie took it and sat down beside her.

"Do you want me to read it?" Maggie asked.

Hannah shook her head. "No. I've got it. I just need a minute."

Maggie kissed her cheek. "It's okay, baby. It's okay. We got this together."

Hannah continued. "Human error. It is believed that human error was at fault. Ms. Walsh's patient number zero-five-nine-eight-six, and Ms. Kennedy's patient number zero-five-nine-eight-nine were very similar. On the day of the procedure, it is our current understanding there was a mix-up in the files and it is believed that one of our staff members supplied the doctor with the wrong embryos. Blah, blah, blah, same sperm donor contributed to the mix-up." Most of the rest of the report was filled with legal mumbo jumbo, the clinic taking no legal responsibility…employee had long ago been let go…they believed the offer was more than fair to make up for any inconvenience the matter caused.

Hannah felt like her heart was now located in her throat and her stomach had been pulled out through her ribs.

"Inconvenience," Maggie said. "Inconvenience? How dare they. This is more than an inconvenience. And what the hell offer are they talking about?" She grabbed the lawyer's letter from the coffee table. "Hannah. This says they are offering us a quarter of a million dollars."

"What?" Hannah didn't know whether to laugh or cry. Or scream, which is what she wanted to do most.

"Each," Maggie continued.

"What?" Hannah repeated. "Is that supposed to make up for what they did? And they take no legal responsibility? How is that right?"

"It isn't. But there is no way they can make this right. They can't rewrite the past any more than we can. The lawyer wants to know if she should accept the offer or if we want to go to court."

Hannah was finding it hard to think. They weren't really going to sue the clinic. They just wanted information and now they had it. Was it right to accept the money they were offering? What would that say about Cassidy? That she was a human error?

"Hannah?"

"We weren't really going to sue."

"I know that. But obviously they didn't. If we accept the money, Cassidy can go to any college she wants to."

"Veterinary college," Hannah said.

"What?"

Hannah looked at Maggie. "She's talked about going to veterinary college. It's another four years after she gets her bachelor's degree. She was worried about the time and the expense. It won't help the time, but it sure as hell could take care of the expense."

Should they take the money if it helped Cassidy? That was a whole different way of looking at this. Cassidy had been the most affected; she should be the one to reap any benefits.

"I think we should accept it," Maggie said. "It won't change anything, but it could make the future a little easier for Cassidy."

Hannah couldn't argue with that. She would be a fool to say no and deny Cassidy a better future. "Okay," she said.

"Okay?"

"Yes. Okay. Let's do this. Let's make a better future for our girl."

❖

Cassidy did well enough with her jumping lessons that Maggie relented and allowed her to enter the competition at the fairgrounds.

Maggie parked the truck in the designated lot on the fairgrounds and Cassidy helped her unload Clover from the horse trailer. Maggie was more nervous than Cassidy appeared to be.

Cassidy seemed to be bubbling over with excitement. She was dressed in the traditional white pants, white-collar shirt, and long boots. She had her safety helmet and dark jacket in her backpack.

"You're sure you want to do this? You really think you're ready?" Maggie rubbed Cassidy's shoulder.

"I am sooo ready."

They watched the first riders go through the course with near perfection.

Cassidy was up next.

"Remember what I taught you. This isn't a race. Pay attention to your posture and rhythm. You and Clover need to work together," Maggie said. "Know ahead of time where you need to start each jump."

"Maggie, I got it. You've told me this stuff a million times."

"Yeah, no. I don't think it was more than five hundred thousand."

Maggie held her breath as Cassidy and Clover cleared the first rail with very little effort. Her posture was spot-on. They made the turn smoothly and jumps number two and three went off without a hitch. Coming up on the fourth jump, Maggie could tell their pace was off and Cassidy started the jump too early.

Maggie clamped her jaw down and sucked in a breath through her lips, waiting to see if they could somehow pull it off.

Clover must have sensed that they weren't going to make it and stopped dead in his tracks.

From where Maggie was standing, it looked like Cassidy smashed her face into Clover's neck before flipping over his head and landing hard on the ground in front of the rails.

Maggie was by her side in a flash. She wasn't even sure her feet had touched the ground in her rush to get there. "Don't move," she told her.

Cassidy blinked twice and then lost consciousness. A trickle of blood was coming from her nose. Maggie was about to scream for help when she was pulled backward by her shoulders.

"Back up. Let them do their jobs," someone said to her.

Two men and a woman, paramedics, Maggie reasoned, moved in quickly. Maggie had forgotten that they always had EMTs and an ambulance standing by. They had a collar on Cassidy and had her strapped to a board by the time Cassidy came to.

"Wha—" Cassidy started.

Maggie was by her side as they transferred her to the waiting ambulance. "Shh," she said. "I'm here. Don't try to move."

"Are you her mother?" the female EMT asked her.

"I am," Maggie said. Close enough. "I'm coming with you."

She called Hannah on the ride to the hospital and told her what had happened.

"Is she all right?" Hannah asked.

"She's conscious. They are keeping her still until she can be checked out. That's all I know right now."

Hannah didn't ask anything else and said she would meet them at the hospital. Hannah beat them there and was standing at the entrance to the emergency department when the ambulance pulled in. She rushed to Cassidy's side. "What happened? Are you okay?"

"Ma'am, we need to get her in," the EMT said to her. She stepped back. "I'm sure the doctor will be out soon to give you an update. You can wait in there." He pointed to the left. He turned to Maggie and said, "I'm sure they are going to want you to fill out paperwork. Make sure you check in at the front desk."

"Why are they asking you to do that?" Hannah asked.

"They just assume I'm her mother because I was with her."

"Did you tell them you were?"

"I knew it was the only way they would let me ride in the ambulance with her." And besides I *am* her mother, Maggie thought. I just didn't get to give birth or raise her.

"So yes. You did."

Maggie wanted to calm Hannah down and at the same time wanted to scream in her face, *You aren't the only one who's worried here.*

Hannah went over to the check in desk. Maggie followed.

A bored looking woman slid the glass window open. "Can I help you?"

"My daughter, Cassidy Kennedy, was just brought in by ambulance," Hannah said.

The woman pulled several sheets of paper from various cubbies, slipped them onto a clipboard, and handed it to Hannah. "Fill this out. Pens are in the cup to your left. Bring it back up when you're done." She slid the window closed again.

Maggie sat helplessly by as Hannah filled out the papers and returned them to the window.

Hannah pulled Maggie off to the side of the waiting room. "What the hell were you thinking?"

"I..." Maggie struggled to explain.

"You weren't thinking. Otherwise you would never have talked Cassidy into this."

"I didn't talk her into anything."

"Well, you did something, because she is in that room with God knows what broken. I should have known not to trust you from the moment I found out you came into my floral shop and never told me who you were."

Maggie thought of several things she could say in retaliation but decided that attacking back wasn't a good idea. "That's not fair," she said.

"It's not fair that Cassidy has to go through this." Hannah's spit her words at Maggie like venom. "Tell me exactly what happened."

"Let's sit down and I'll explain everything." Maggie led them over to a couple of empty chairs away from everyone else. "Cassidy started taking show jumping lessons from me several weeks ago."

"And you never thought to mention this to me? It's not like we haven't been seeing each other on a regular basis."

Maggie didn't want to throw Cassidy under the bus, but she thought honesty was the best way to go. "Cassidy asked me not to. She wanted to surprise you. To make you proud."

"Proud? Proud that she is here? Hurt?" Hannah's anger didn't seem to be subsiding. "You should have told me."

"Hannah, I never thought for one minute Cassidy would get hurt. I would never do anything that I thought would put her in danger. Never."

Hannah couldn't believe that Maggie did this. Teaching Cassidy behind her back was bad enough but having her compete and keeping it from her was a whole other level of deceit. Hannah just prayed that Cassidy would be all right. There would be no forgiving Maggie if she wasn't.

"Cassidy was doing really well with the lessons. I made sure she knew what she was doing before I let her compete," Maggie said.

"Then what happened? Because she obviously wasn't ready."

"She started a jump too soon and the horse stopped instead of taking a jump he knew wouldn't work. He stopped and the momentum sent Cassidy over his head."

"Oh my God. You should have protected her from this. I never wanted her to compete with the jumping. She knew that." She knew that, but Hannah guessed that didn't matter when Maggie was willing to teach her. Hannah knew that at eighteen, Cassidy was old enough to make her own decision, but damn it, why did she have to do this? The one thing Hannah didn't want her to do.

"Hannah, I thought she was ready."

A nurse came out through the doors separating the waiting room from the patient area. "Who's here with Cassidy Kennedy?"

Hannah was on her feet in an instant. "Is she all right?" She made her way over to the nurse.

"The doctor is still with her. I'll bring you back to there."

Maggie was right behind them. Hannah wasn't about to make a scene by telling her she couldn't come with them. And the nurse didn't seem to mind that she was there.

A gray-haired man with a stethoscope around his neck was standing next to the bed as they entered the cubicle. He shook hands with Hannah and then Maggie. "I'm Dr. Jackson."

"Which one of you is Cassidy's mother?"

Maggie opened her mouth to say something, but Hannah answered before she had the chance. "I am," Hannah said.

Hannah went to Cassidy's side. She was awake and looked somewhat alert but pale. A purple bruise was starting to form on her cheek and a bit of dried blood clung to her upper lip. "Are you all right, honey?" Hannah asked her.

She nodded, winced, and rubbed her forehead.

"Nothing broken," the doctor started. "But she does have a mild concussion. She can expect headaches and problems with concentration and short-term memory for several days. Balance and coordination problems can also occur. Your paperwork will have a complete list of other possible symptoms. Absolutely no physical activity as long as she is having symptoms. I recommend she wait at least a couple of weeks after they resolve completely before engaging in any sports or exercise." He tapped Cassidy on the knee. "And that includes horseback riding, young lady."

Hannah knew a concussion wasn't good, but it could have been so much worse. What the hell was Maggie thinking, she wondered once again.

"It isn't unusual for a person to not remember the event that led to the concussion for several days. Sometimes they never regain that memory," Dr. Jackson said.

That would explain the confused look on Cassidy's face as she listened to the doctor.

"When can she go home?" Hannah asked him.

"We'd like to keep her for about an hour and a half more, just to be on the safe side. She can go home after that. It would be a good idea to keep her quiet for the next few days. She should rest as much as possible. Do you have someone that can stay with her?"

"I can, if you can't," Maggie said to Hannah. "Randi can handle the lessons for the next few days."

Hannah didn't like that idea, but she had a big order for a wedding she had to prepare. Becca could help, but she certainly couldn't handle it on her own. Maybe Sarah could stay with Cassidy. "Yes. We'll have someone with her."

"Good. Like I said, her discharge papers will have more information about concussions. Tylenol as needed. No other types of pain medication. Do you have any questions?"

"Why am I here?" Cassidy asked.

The doctor turned his attention to her. "It's my understanding that you had a little accident with a horse. Do you remember it at all?"

She shook her head and winced.

He turned his attention to Hannah. "Like I said that's not at all unusual. Her memory of the incident may come back or it may not." He turned back to Cassidy. "The most important thing is that you are going to be just fine. But you need to take it easy for a while. Can you do that for me?"

"I think so."

"You can wait in here with her if you want. Or go get something to eat." He looked at his watch. "I'll have her discharge papers ready by four."

"I'll stay with her," Hannah said.

"I'll have someone bring in another chair." The doctor looked at each of them and left.

"You don't need to stay," Hannah said to Maggie. She knew it was harsh. She also knew that Maggie probably didn't deserve it, but damn it. Cassidy got hurt on Maggie's watch.

"I want to stay."

"I want her to stay," Cassidy said. "What happened? Why am I here?"

Hannah pulled the one chair in the room over to the side of the bed and sat. She took Cassidy's hand in hers. "You had an accident," Hannah said. "But the doctor said you'll be just fine."

"A car accident?" Cassidy asked.

Maggie made her way over to the other side of the bed. "No, honey. You were competing in show jumping and you went over Clover's head and landed on the ground."

"Is Clover okay?" Cassidy asked.

"I'm sure he's fine, honey. You don't need to worry about him."

"Did I mess up?" Cassidy asked.

"What?" Hannah asked.

"Did I mess up with Clover?" She turned her attention back to Maggie. "I must have done something wrong. Clover wouldn't have thrown me. It had to be something I did."

Maggie looked at Hannah. Hannah knew the silent questions she was asking, and she nodded her approval.

Maggie explained what had happened to Cassidy.

"I'm so sorry, Maggie," Cassidy said.

"Oh no. You don't need to be sorry. These things happen. I'm just happy that you're okay."

"How come my head hurts?" Cassidy asked.

"You have a concussion," Hannah told her.

"I do?"

"Yes. And you need to take it easy for the next few days."

Cassidy asked why she was there and what happened two more times before the nurse arrived with her discharge papers.

Hannah took the nurse aside. "She has asked several times what happened. She can't seem to retain the information for more than a few minutes."

"That's totally normal with a concussion. Did the doctor go over that with you?"

Hannah nodded. "Yes. But it's—"

"Worrisome. I know. But truly, it's to be expected. It will resolve itself. It could be tonight, or it might take a day or two. Try not to worry."

Easier said than done. Hannah was her mother. Worry was part of the job description.

"You can help her get dressed and I'll be back with a wheelchair," the nurse said.

"I can walk," Cassidy said.

"Hospital rules," the nurse said, and was gone.

It didn't take long for Cassidy to be dressed in her riding attire. Hannah considered leaving her boots off but decided it wouldn't be a good idea for Cassidy to walk from the wheelchair to the car or into the house barefooted.

Hannah went to get the car while Maggie stayed with Cassidy. It didn't take long for them to appear at the emergency department door, the nurse pushing the wheelchair, with Maggie close behind.

Hannah put the car in park, jumped out, and helped Cassidy get into the passenger seat. She looked up at Maggie standing on the curb, by the car. "I've got it from here. You can go home." She silently reprimanded herself, but she couldn't seem to be civil to Maggie. Her anger was still too close to the surface.

Maggie just stood there making no attempt to move. It was then that Hannah remembered that her car must be wherever the competition was. Shit. Hannah was tempted to leave her standing there. She could just take a taxi or an Uber or ride a cow for all Hannah cared.

Cassidy rolled down her window. "Do you need a ride, Maggie?"

Maggie looked at Hannah.

Dammit. "Whatever. Get in. I'll get you back to your car." Hannah knew she was being a bitch and in that moment she didn't care.

I can't believe Hannah is being such a bitch. Maggie knew she would be upset over Cassidy getting hurt, but this was just way too much. She considered turning down the ride, but she *did* need to get back to her truck and to Clover. "Thanks. I appreciate it." She climbed into the back seat.

"Where am I going?" Hannah asked her.

Maggie told her where the competition was and offered her directions.

"I know how to get there."

They were silent on the ride back to the fairgrounds. Not the comfortable quiet that they often shared. No, this was more like a tortured silence. Like every second seemed like an hour.

"Thank you for the ride," Maggie said as she got out of the car. She leaned into the still open back door. "Please keep me updated. Let me know later how she's doing. My offer to stay with her still stands. I'll talk to Randi tonight about taking over the lessons for the rest of this week."

Hannah just nodded.

"Bye, Cassidy. Follow the doctor's orders and take it easy."

Maggie closed the door and watched Hannah drive away. She had a sudden desire to punch something. Or someone. Fuck. Fuck. Fuck. Not only had Cassidy gotten hurt, something she blamed herself for, but Hannah was a jerk about it. She didn't see how they could recover from this. Hannah would probably never forgive her. Hell, she would probably never forgive herself.

Maggie thought of all the things she could have said to hurt Hannah back. Hannah had asked her to keep a couple of secrets from Cassidy as well. What the hell was the difference? But Maggie hadn't said anything about that. She didn't want to hurt Hannah back. She wanted to hug her. But that wasn't a possibility. And that made Maggie sad. She'd never seen Hannah so mad. And to be the object of that anger was heartbreaking.

She went into the building and found it nearly empty. Luckily, one of the show organizers recognized her right away. "How's the girl, Cassidy?" the well-dressed woman asked.

"Concussion. But she'll be okay. She just needs to take it easy for a while." Maggie laughed. It was sad and a bit sarcastic. "I think the hardest part for her will be not being able to ride until she heals. She eats and breathes horses."

"David took care of her horse. I'm assuming you're here to get it."

Maggie nodded. "Where can I find him?"

The woman pointed the way and Maggie headed in that direction. Clover was still saddled, in a makeshift stall. He was agitated, like he knew what he had done and was sorry. Maggie ran a hand over his neck in an attempt to calm him down. "It's okay, boy. You didn't mean it. I know you didn't. I'm sure she'll forgive you. Let's go home. We both had one hell of a day, didn't we?"

She took him outside, took off his saddle and gear, and led him up the ramp to the horse trailer. She reassured him one more time before closing the door and throwing the saddle in the back of her truck. She sent a text to Randi, letting her know what had happened and asking if she could cover the chores and lessons for the next several days in case she needed to stay with Cassidy. She promised to double her pay. Randi said of course she could.

Clover didn't settle down until they were home and he was in his own stall. She gave him fresh food and water, checked that Randi had taken care of everything else, and headed out of the barn. She closed the barn door, leaned against it, and slid to the ground.

All the emotions of the day poured out of her as the tears rolled down her cheeks and sobs escaped her throat. She was glad no one was around to witness it. She was spent by the time she pulled herself up, headed to the house, and went inside.

She paused in the living room on the way to her bathroom and stared at the couch. The place where she'd first made love to Hannah. More tears ran down her cheeks. "I hope to God that it's not over," she said out loud to the empty room.

She continued to the bathroom, stripped off her clothes, and climbed into the shower. The hot water mixed with her tears and ran down the drain as if they didn't exist.

She replayed the day in her mind. It had started out so good. Cassidy had been so excited. And Maggie thought she was ready. She really did. They'd walked the course and discussed the plan. Maggie didn't know if it was nerves or lack of experience, but Cassidy starting that fourth jump too soon caused Clover to stop.

She didn't blame Cassidy. She blamed herself. Hannah was right. It was her fault. Not teaching Cassidy how to jump. That's not where her mistake was. It was in not telling Hannah and letting Cassidy compete too soon. Yes. She could be blamed for those things. Not only was Cassidy hurt, but she may have lost Hannah in the process. She didn't blame Hannah for hating her. She was hating on herself just as much. Maybe more.

She hoped Cassidy could forgive her. She didn't know if Hannah ever would. Forgiving herself would be the hardest of them all.

She toweled off, made her way to her bedroom, and threw herself on her bed, not bothering to put anything on, or even pulling back the covers. She deserved to freeze her ass off as she slept—assuming she could sleep at all.

CHAPTER SIXTEEN

Hannah called Sarah as soon as she dropped Maggie off and told her what had happened. "Can you stay with her the next couple of days while I'm at work? I have a huge order for a wedding that I need to put together."

"Oh, honey, I'm so sorry I can't. We are doing inventory at work this week and it's mandatory that we be there. We should be done by three. I can come straight over then."

"Let me try Linda and Mom. If they can't do it, I'll text you."

"Good luck. Please keep me updated on how Cassidy is doing. Love you."

Linda wasn't available either, neither was her mother nor the couple of friends that she called.

"Shit," Hannah said as she pulled into the driveway. She sent Sarah a text asking her to come over after work the next day.

"What's the matter, Mom?"

"Nothing, honey. I just need to find someone to stay with you for a couple of days while I work."

"Why? I've been staying home alone since I was a little kid."

Hannah laughed. "Well, that's not quite true, but remember the doctor said you have a concussion and we should have someone with you for the next couple of days."

"I do?"

"Yes."

"How?"

Hannah gave her a brief explanation of what had happened.

"Was I wearing a helmet? Maggie said I always have to wear a helmet, even when I'm just practicing."

"I imagine you were. But you hit your head pretty hard. Let's go in and get you something to eat."

After a quick sandwich and two Tylenol, Hannah helped Cassidy get ready for bed and settled her in for the night. She left Cassidy's and her own bedroom doors open, stretched out on her bed, and took a few deep breaths, willing her tense muscles to loosen up. It had been an intense few hours.

She stared at Maggie's contact info on her phone. She'd run out of options and needed Maggie to stay with Cassidy while she was at the shop.

Yeah, she had been hard on her at the hospital. Maybe too hard. But Maggie had no right keeping the competition a secret from her, no matter what Cassidy had asked her to do. And Cassidy got hurt. Those things added up to Hannah getting all *mama bear* in attack mode.

She typed. *If you were serious can you stay with Cassidy tomorrow from eight thirty am till about three thirty? My sister can stay with her after that until I get home.*

It took so long for Maggie to answer that Hannah thought she wasn't going to. When her phone finally pinged, Maggie's response was simple. *I'll be there.*

Hannah started to type *thank you*, changed her mind, and threw her phone on the bed. Yeah, she was pissed, and she was going to stay pissed, as long as she damn well pleased.

❖

The doorbell rang ten minutes before eight thirty the next morning. Hannah was exhausted from trying to sleep—without really sleeping—so she could hear Cassidy if she got up during the night. She'd checked on her no less than ten times. Each time, she stood in Cassidy's doorway watching her until she was sure she was breathing.

Hannah set her coffee down and went to the door. She took a deep breath before opening it, trying to calm the anger that still took up residence in her gut. "Hi, Maggie. Thanks for coming."

"Of course. How's our—" Maggie stopped. "How's Cassidy?"

"She slept through the night. I was just about to wake her up. There's coffee in the pot in the kitchen. Or I can make you tea when I come back down." Hannah disappeared up the stairs.

Maggie made her way to the kitchen. She found a cup in the second cabinet she opened and poured herself a cup of coffee. Tea was her morning beverage of choice, but this morning she would settle for coffee. Best not to cause any kind of fuss. She sniffed the carton of milk, more out of habit than anything else, and added a fair amount to her cup.

"Hi, Maggie." Cassidy, still in her pajamas, came into the kitchen, followed closely by Hannah. "What are you doing here?"

"Hi, Cass. I thought maybe we could spend the day together. How are you feeling?"

"I'm okay, except for this headache." She rubbed her forehead.

"Got your Tylenol right here," Hannah said. She handed her a couple of pills and got her a glass of water. "Maggie's going to stay with you while I go to work, then Aunt Sarah will be here. I probably won't be home until six o'clock." She turned to Maggie. "She still doesn't remember anything about yesterday. I explained to her again about the concussion and that she has to take it easy."

"Okay," Maggie replied.

Hannah poured the rest of her coffee from her cup into a travel mug and added more from the pot. She explained what there was for breakfast and lunch. "Remote is in front of the television. You have my number if there are any problems. My sister will be here shortly after three."

"We'll be fine," Maggie said.

Hannah rubbed Cassidy's shoulder. "Need anything before I go?"

Cassidy shook her head.

"Okay. I'll see you later, honey." She grabbed her coffee and an apple from the bowl on the counter. "Maggie, help yourself to anything you want. There's different kinds of tea in the cupboard."

"Thanks," Maggie said. She had only been in Hannah's house a couple of times and that was just to pick Cassidy up. Every time they got together it was either at Maggie's place or out in public. Maggie figured that was so they could keep their relationship a secret. It was a different secret that got them to this place now. A secret Maggie never should have agreed to keep.

Hannah stopped, seemed to take inventory to make sure she had everything, and was out the door.

Maggie made Cassidy eggs and toast and sat with her while she ate.

"Mom said I got hurt jumping Clover," Cassidy said between bites.

"You don't remember any of it?"

"No. How did I do up until then? Did I make all the jumps?"

Maggie shook her head. "You made the first three jumps like a champ." She paused, not sure how much she should say.

"Go on. I want to know what happened. It's not fun having gaps in your memory. I'm assuming I fell. Why? What did I do wrong?"

"You sure you want to hear this?"

Cassidy nodded. "If I don't know what I messed up how am I going to learn from it and make sure I don't make the same mistake again?"

"You still want to jump? Even after getting hurt?" Maggie asked.

"Absolutely. I love it."

"You need to get your mother's blessing if we are going to continue with the lessons. She's not too happy with me right now."

"Why? It was my idea," Cassidy said.

Maggie was sorry she'd said that. No sense putting Cassidy in the middle of it. "Never mind. You want to know about the jump that went wrong?"

"Yeah."

"Your pace was off. You started the jump too soon. Remember I told you that if that happened, Clover might refuse the jump, or he might go around the rails?"

"Yes. I'm assuming he didn't go around it."

"Nope. He stopped very suddenly right before the rail and you went over his head. You hit the ground pretty hard."

"I had a helmet on, right? How come I still got a concussion?"

"A helmet can only do so much, honey. Hit hard enough and your brain still gets a good shaking."

"Why is Mom mad at you?"

Shit. "Forget I said that," Maggie said.

"You didn't have to say anything. I could tell." Hannah must still be really pissed for Cassidy to have noticed.

Maggie struggled for an answer that wasn't really *the* answer. "She's just worried about you. I am too, to tell you the truth. It was pretty scary."

"I'm fine. You don't need to worry." Cassidy finished her breakfast and pushed her plate forward.

Maggie cleaned up the kitchen and they settled down together in the living room. They binged old episodes of *Friends* until it was time for lunch. Cassidy only ate half of the sandwich Maggie made her. Maggie slipped the rest into a Ziploc bag and put it in the fridge in case Cassidy wanted it later. She gave Cassidy two more Tylenol and a glass of water.

"Drink the whole glass," Maggie said. "We don't want you getting dehydrated on top of everything else now. Do we?"

Cassidy fell asleep on the couch during the second round of their *Friends* marathon. She was still asleep when Sarah arrived, letting herself in.

"You must be Maggie," Sarah whispered.

Maggie nodded, got up, and led the way to the kitchen. Better to let Cassidy sleep. Rest was the best thing for her healing. "Sarah, right?"

"Yes. I'm Hannah's sister. How is our little patient in there?" She cocked her thumb in the direction of the living room.

"She's a trooper." Maggie filled her in on the details. "So, she can have more medicine at five if her headache comes back. Would you like some coffee, or I can make tea?" Maggie felt a little funny playing hostess in Hannah's house.

"I can get it," Sarah said. "Would you like a cup of tea as well?"

"Why don't you sit and let me get it?" Maggie said. "I'm sure you've been working all day. You must be tired." Maggie filled the tea kettle and set it back on the stove, turning the burner up high. She listed the various teas in the cupboard, pulled out the black raspberry tea for Sarah and the hibiscus for herself. She leaned back against the counter while she waited for the water to heat up.

"I've heard a lot about you," Sarah started. "Hannah mentioned you were dating."

Guess we were only a secret from Cassidy, Maggie thought.

"Hannah is quite taken with you."

Not anymore. Maggie was at a loss for words. Obviously, Hannah hadn't told Sarah her latest feelings. "I think she's pretty special," Maggie said at last. "Kind of an unusual situation that brought us together."

"To say the least," Sarah said.

"I've heard Hannah's side of it. Finding out that Cassidy wasn't her biological child. I would be interested to hear how you're feeling about it. Please stop me if my questions are too personal. I don't mean to pry."

It hadn't even occurred to Maggie that Sarah was prying. Like Hannah, she seemed genuinely interested in her feelings. She could tell they were sisters. "It was a shock for sure. But I have to say that I am glad Cassidy is in this world and that it was Hannah who brought her into it. I couldn't have asked for a better mother for Cassidy, even if I'd picked her out myself."

"I have to agree with that. Hannah is the best. I'm so glad you two—you three—all found each other."

The tea kettle started its whistle and Maggie jumped to turn it off before it woke up Cassidy. She prepared two cups of tea and checked on Cassidy—who was still fast asleep. She settled down across from Sarah. Maggie could see why Hannah confided in her. She seemed like a really caring, genuine person.

"Will you be back here tomorrow?" Sarah asked.

"I'm not sure. I cleared my schedule, but Hannah hasn't told me if she needs me tomorrow or not." She sipped her tea, found it to be a little too hot, and set it back down to cool.

"I take it the doctor wants someone with Cassidy for at least a couple of days. I think Hannah has to work tomorrow too. I can come about three twenty tomorrow again."

"Will you ask her to text me when she gets home to let me know?"

A look of confusion flashed across Sarah's face for a moment.

Maggie figured she must have wondered why Maggie didn't just ask Hannah herself. Good question. Why didn't Maggie just ask her herself? Yeah, Hannah was mad at her. But Maggie didn't have to act like there was any kind of a problem between them. "Never mind. I'll text her later." If there was going to be any fixing this—and Maggie prayed there was—they needed to keep the lines of communication open. Maggie was willing to do her part. All she could do was hope Hannah would do hers.

"How's it going?" Hannah asked as she walked into the living room.

Sarah and Cassidy were on the couch together, some movie playing on the TV. Cassidy had her feet curled up underneath her.

Sarah hit the mute button on the remote. "Good. Cassidy took a nice nap earlier. I think she's feeling a little better. Isn't that right, Cassidy?"

Cassidy looked at Hannah. She did look a little less spacey than she did when Hannah left. The dark rings under her eyes looked a little lighter. "Yep. I feel better. Not great. But better."

"That's good." Hannah went into the kitchen to rinse out her travel mug.

Sarah followed. "I really like Maggie. I can see why you're attracted to her."

Hannah didn't respond. She put her mug in the dish drain.

"Hannah?"

"What?" She turned toward her sister.

"Did you hear me?"

"I did. I'm really mad at her right now."

Sarah pulled out a chair and sat. She patted the table silently telling Hannah to join her. "Why? What did she do?"

Hannah sat. "She gave Cassidy jumping lessons behind my back. And then she…she…" Hannah waved her hand in the air. "She let her enter this competition, again without telling me, and Cassidy got hurt." Hannah tried to keep her voice down, but it came out louder and sounding angrier than she had intended.

"Hannah, Cassidy is old enough to take lessons without your permission. How come Maggie didn't tell you about them?"

Sarah's response only managed to fuel Hannah's anger.

"I know she's old enough. That's not the point. Maggie should have told me. Cassidy asked her not to because she wanted to surprise me." Hannah used air quotes around the word *surprise*.

"I'm still not seeing a problem here. I'm sure Maggie was devastated when Cassidy got hurt. She wouldn't have let her compete if she didn't think she was ready. And as far as not telling you, well, you didn't tell Cassidy that you were taking lessons or even that you were seeing Maggie."

"My dating Maggie has nothing to do with this."

"What?" Cassidy appeared in the doorway. "You're dating Maggie?"

Oh crap. This was not the way she wanted Cassidy to find out. And now that it was probably over, there had been no need for her to find out at all.

Sarah mouthed the words *I'm sorry*.

"I was," Hannah said to Cassidy. "But not anymore."

"I don't understand. All those times you were out. You were with Maggie?"

Hannah let out a breath before answering. "Yes."

"And you didn't tell me? Why?"

Did any of this matter now? Hannah wasn't so sure anymore.

"Why?" Cassidy repeated.

Anger rose in Hannah's chest. She rubbed the back of her neck and shook her head. "Why didn't you tell me you were taking jumping lessons? You knew I didn't want you to."

"I didn't tell you because I wanted to surprise you. I wanted you to be proud of me. And Maggie is an expert so I thought you would be fine if it was her teaching me. I never thought it would be a problem. Ever." Some of the color drained from Cassidy's face.

Hannah was on her feet in a split second, pulling out a chair for her. "Sit down. You're getting yourself all worked up." Hannah got her a glass of water.

Cassidy sat and took a couple of sips.

"We don't need to talk about this now," Hannah said. Or ever.

Cassidy set the glass on the table. "I think we do. Why didn't you tell me about Maggie and you?"

"I didn't want to upset you and I didn't know where it was going. I figured if it didn't work out, then there would be no reason to tell you," Hannah said, consciously keeping her voice calm. She hoped that answered Cassidy's question enough that they could drop it.

"I'm *more* upset about you keeping it from me than the fact that you were dating," Cassidy said.

"And can you see why I'm upset that you and Maggie didn't tell me about the jumping lessons?"

"Mom, I wanted to surprise you, not deceive you. Don't tell me you kept that from me for the same reason."

"I wasn't trying to deceive you, Cassidy. I was trying to protect you."

"From what?" Cassidy wasn't making this easy. "From Maggie?"

"No. But I never should have trusted Maggie." Hannah regretted saying that as soon as it was out of her mouth. She really didn't want to upset Cassidy, especially with a concussion.

"Why? I don't understand any of this. What did she do that was so bad?"

"Cassidy, let's not—" Hannah started.

"No," Cassidy interrupted her. "You aren't going to blow this off. I'm not a little kid. I have a right to know what's going on."

Hannah glanced at Sarah, silently asking if she should explain. Sarah shrugged. She was no help.

"Maggie never should have given you lessons or brought you to a competition without talking to me first."

"Why?" Cassidy asked.

"Because I'm your mother."

"I..." Cassidy tapped her chest a few times. "I asked her to teach me and not tell you. Don't blame Maggie for that. If that is the reason you aren't dating her anymore then you're wrong."

"Not my business." Sarah put her hands up. "But I'm with Cassidy. Seems you both kept your secrets. You didn't even tell Cassidy about taking riding lessons with Maggie." Her eyes went wide. "Shit. Didn't mean to say that."

"Thanks," Hannah said to Sarah.

"So sorry. I'm going to go." Sarah stood. "Call me later." She left before Hannah had a chance to respond.

Cassidy shook her head. "This is crazy. Sounds like we all had secrets we were keeping."

"I'm sorry I didn't tell you about that. I thought you would like it if I could ride with you sometimes. It wasn't supposed to be a secret forever."

"And neither was my secret. If you want to blame someone, blame me," Cassidy said.

Hannah realized just how mature her daughter was. But Cassidy wasn't the only one involved in this. Maggie still held a good deal of the blame.

"I don't want to fight about this," Hannah said. "Why don't you go into the living room and rest while I make dinner."

"I've been resting all day," Cassidy responded.

"You are *supposed* to be resting all day. So good job. Do you need more Tylenol?"

Cassidy got up. "No." She stormed out of the kitchen.

Well, that didn't go well. Shit. Guess there were no more secrets between them. At least Hannah hoped there weren't. She had just put the spaghetti in the pot of boiling water when her phone pinged. The text from Maggie asked how Cassidy was doing and if she was needed tomorrow.

Hannah responded with a brief update on Cassidy and told her yes, she needed her to stay with Cassidy again. She wished she didn't need her help, but she did. Damn it all to hell.

Chapter Seventeen

How are you feeling today?" Maggie asked Cassidy over breakfast the next morning.

"Better." Cassidy poured syrup on her pancakes. She set the bottle down and put her attention on Maggie. "I know about you and Mom."

Maggie's mouth dropped open. "You do? Your mom told you?"

Cassidy shook her head. "No. I'm sure she didn't want me to know. I overheard her and Aunt Sarah talking."

Maggie resisted the urge to ask exactly what they said. She was sure it wouldn't be too flattering. Not with the way Hannah was feeling about her.

"I would have been okay with it, you know." Cassidy stuffed a piece of pancake in her mouth.

"Did you tell your mom that?" Maggie asked.

Cassidy took her time chewing and swallowing. "She didn't really give me a chance. I'm pretty sure she didn't want to talk about it."

Maggie wasn't surprised. She wondered if Hannah said they were over. She didn't want to ask. She waited, but Cassidy didn't volunteer any other information.

The rest of the day went pretty much like the first day, except they watched far less TV and spent part of the day sitting outside. Maggie made sure Cassidy sat in the shade.

They were still in the backyard when Sarah arrived and joined them out back. She unfolded one of the lawn chairs leaning against the house and sat with them. They made small talk until Maggie got up to leave.

"I'll walk you out," Sarah said. "Cassidy, you okay here for a few minutes?"

"I'm fine. I'm not sure why everyone is making such a big deal out of this," she answered.

"I'll take that as a yes," Sarah said. She followed Maggie to the front door. "How are you doing?"

Maggie was confused. "I'm all right." She hesitated. "Why are you asking?"

"Because I like you and I know you've been through a lot the last few days. Hell, for weeks. I get the feeling Hannah is..." Sarah paused.

"Pissed as hell?" Maggie filled in.

"That's a little stronger than I would have put it, but yeah. I get the feeling she's mad."

"I'm getting that feeling too. I'm not sure what to do about it. I hate this. I've tried to explain, but she doesn't seem to want to listen." Maggie chose her words carefully. She didn't want to make Hannah sound like the bad guy in this. "I care about her so much."

"I know you do. She's worth fighting for. I get the feeling you are too. The only suggestion I have is don't give up. Hang in there."

"I don't think there's anything to hang on to anymore." Maggie's eyes filled with tears. The last thing she wanted to do was cry in front of Hannah's sister. She blinked, willing her tears to stay put. "I better get going," Maggie said. She turned so Sarah couldn't see the tears that refused her orders.

She was a few blocks away when she pulled the car over and allowed herself to cry. She banged her fists on the steering wheel as sobs escaped her throat. For a little while she'd had it all, a daughter, a lover, a life she hadn't dared dream of. She still had Cassidy. For now. She could only hope that Hannah didn't turn Cassidy against her. That felt like the only hope she had left.

❖

"No. We are not going there," Hannah said to Sarah. "Where's Cassidy?" It had been a long day at the floral shop. Hannah was in no mood for a lecture.

"She's sitting out back. She's fine," Sarah said. "I'm just saying I think Maggie is hurting."

"She's not the only one."

"And *you* can fix it, so no one hurts."

"Cassidy hurts. She hit her head so hard that she has a concussion. She can't do *anything* she wants to. No working. No horses. No riding. Don't tell me that doesn't hurt her."

"Cassidy being grounded is temporary."

"That doesn't make any of this right." Hannah started for the back door.

"Hannah, I'm not done."

Hannah turned to look at her sister. "I think you are. You're free to join us for dinner if you want. I'm going to check on my kid." She started again toward the backyard.

"She's not a kid," Sarah called after her.

Hannah turned around.

"She's not a kid anymore. I think that's what the problem is here," Sarah said.

"What is that supposed to mean?" Hannah took several steps back toward her sister, anger seeping in around the edges.

"It means she can make decisions for herself. Even decisions that you don't like. You are still treating her like a child and Maggie didn't."

"Maybe if Maggie had, Cassidy wouldn't be in this condition." Great. The whole world seemed like it was against her. All she was trying to do was protect her kid—Cassidy. Okay, maybe she wasn't a kid anymore, but a mother never stopped trying to protect her offspring. Offspring? Cassidy wasn't even that. Was she? It was all so confusing. All so frustrating.

"Oh, come on, Hannah. Who are you really mad at here?" Sarah asked.

"I'm mad at Maggie." She paused to think. "And I'm mad at myself for trusting her."

"What exactly did she do to betray that trust? She didn't cheat on you. She didn't lie to you. She kept a secret Cassidy asked her to keep—for a little while. Did she even know you didn't want Cassidy jumping?"

"I don't know." She'd never bothered to ask. "What difference does that make?"

"It makes all the difference in the world."

"She still should have told me." Hannah realized that saying it over and over again was making it lose some of its power.

"You keep telling yourself that. See how far it gets you. You'll be the loser in the end." Sarah turned and walked out the door, slamming it behind her.

Hannah stood there for several long moments staring at the closed door.

"Mom? What are you doing?" She hadn't heard Cassidy come up behind her.

Hannah turned around. "Just trying to figure out life, baby."

"And the answer is in the door?"

"Maybe. How ya doing, kiddo—Cassidy?"

"I'm okay. But you're acting weird. Weirder than normal, I mean."

Hannah forced a laughed. "I'll try to tone it down to my normal range of weird. Come on into the kitchen and keep me company while I make dinner. Unless you want to make it. I've had a hard day at work."

"Sorry." Cassidy pointed to her head. "Concussion or brain damage or something. I'm pretty sure the doctor said no chores for at least a month, maybe longer."

"I'll give you brain damage all right. You can peel the potatoes. That shouldn't stress your brain too much. You can even sit at the table to do it."

"Mom, I think I'm good enough to stay by myself tomorrow," Cassidy said as she put the last peeled potato in the pot.

"You don't want Maggie to come?"

"It's not that. I thought maybe I could go to Horizon tomorrow. I know I'm not supposed to go back to work yet, but I thought maybe I could just help with the lessons from the sidelines."

Hannah wiped her hands on a dishtowel. "No way. You are not driving for at least a week, and you aren't going anywhere near work for at least a couple of weeks. I called them and told them what's going on. You can stay by yourself tomorrow if you promise you won't go anywhere."

"Fine," Cassidy said. "What about college? I'm supposed to go to orientation on Saturday."

Hannah hadn't thought of that. "I have to deliver the flowers for this wedding on Saturday. I'll see if Grandma can take you or one of your aunts. I should be able to join you a little after noon."

"Why can't we ask Maggie?"

Maggie. Maggie would probably want to be there. They hadn't discussed it, although Hannah had planned on asking her to go before everything blew up between them.

"Mom?"

"What?" Hannah realized she'd been lost in her thoughts.

"Maggie?"

"Yes. Fine. Go ahead and ask her. Let me know what she says." Hannah went back to breading the chicken cutlets in front of her.

Her mind vacillated between the way she'd been treating Maggie and what Sarah had to say about it. Was she treating

Cassidy too much like a kid and not giving her space to make her own decisions? Was she holding Maggie responsible for the decisions Cassidy had made? She'd asked Maggie to keep secrets too. Was she justified in doing that? Questions—questions—and more questions. Too many questions and not enough answers.

❖

"I'm so sorry I missed most of orientation," Hannah said. "I had to make some last-minute changes to the floral arrangements for that wedding. I was kind of dealing with the bride from hell."

Maggie hadn't seen Hannah in close to a week. She'd missed her, but it wasn't until that moment that she realized just how much.

"How did it go?" Hannah continued.

"Good," Cassidy answered. "We just have the tour of the campus left. I want to check out the bookstore when we're done."

"Sure. I'd like to get one of those silly mom T-shirts anyway," Hannah said. "I'll get you one too. If you want," she said to Maggie.

"Ah. Um. Yeah." Maggie was at loss for words. Maggie hadn't spoken to her in days other than to text to ask about Cassidy and Hannah had answered them in as few words as possible. And now she was offering to buy her a shirt. And not just any shirt. A mom shirt. What the hell?

"We need to meet by the fountain in—" Cassidy looked at her phone. "Five minutes. I think we should head in that direction now."

"Lead the way," Hannah told her.

The tour of the campus only took about a half hour. That was one good thing about a community college, it wasn't huge.

The bookstore was bigger than Maggie could have imagined. Cassidy went off in search of some college thing or other as soon as they walked in, leaving Hannah and Maggie alone. Well, alone surrounded by about thirty other parents and students milling about.

Hannah pulled a T-shirt off a nearby rack and held it up in front of her. "How about this one?" she asked Maggie.

"My kid went to college and all I got was this lousy T-shirt. Because it's the only thing I can afford now," Maggie read out loud. "Cute."

"Me or the shirt?" Hannah asked.

What? Now she was flirting? She was cold as ice a week ago and now this? Maggie didn't know whether to be happy or mad. But she was definitely leaning more toward being angry. She decided to ignore the question and Hannah. She walked over to another rack and started thumbing through the shirts.

Hannah slipped in between her and the clothes. She looked up, directly into Maggie's eyes for several long beats without saying anything.

Maggie was more confused as ever. "What?" she asked.

Hannah lowered her eyes and then brought them back up. "I'm sorry."

Now it was Maggie who stood there silently.

"I was wrong to blame you. I've done a lot of thinking these past several days and I realized I was wrong, and I treated you very poorly. I hope you can forgive me."

"Okay." Maggie didn't know what else to say. She felt like she'd been yo-yoed all over the place by Hannah. And now she was asking for forgiveness. Maggie wasn't sure she was ready to give it. Hannah had put her through hell with her silent treatment.

"Okay," Hannah repeated and stepped out of Maggie's way.

Maggie continued around the circular rack pretending to look at shirts, but not really registering anything written on them. As much as she had hoped for some sort of sign from Hannah that she was forgiven, or even an acknowledgement that Maggie wasn't the asshole Hannah made her out to be, now she didn't know what to do with it. She felt so empty inside.

❖

Hannah was lost in her own thoughts on the ride home. She'd apologized to Maggie, but it didn't seem to make any difference. Not that she blamed Maggie. She'd been rude—downright mean to her. She'd been so upset over Cassidy getting hurt that it blinded her to the truth. The truth that Maggie cared about Cassidy and would never do anything she thought would harm her. And as for the secret, hell, Hannah could also understand the reason behind that, too.

The question was, what should she do now? And what did she want now? Okay, that was two questions. The answer to the second one was easy. She wanted Maggie back. She just wasn't sure how to get her back. She'd messed things up quite badly. Maybe she didn't deserve a second chance, but she sure as hell wanted one.

"Did you end up getting a shirt?" Cassidy asked.

Hannah blinked a few times, trying to clear her thoughts enough to answer Cassidy's question. "I did."

"What does it say?"

"Something about my smart kid going to college. I forgot exactly."

Cassidy laughed. "You just bought it twenty minutes ago and you forgot already?"

"Hey. My kid is going to college. I have a lot on my mind."

"It's not like you are going to be an empty nester. Yet. I'll be home for a least another year. You know sophomores get to live on campus, don't you?"

Hannah looked at her for a moment before turning her attention back to the road. "I do. I'm not looking forward to that time."

"Why? You'll be free. You can come and go as you please. No one to worry about but you."

"It doesn't matter if you are eight or eighteen or eighty, Cassidy. I will always worry about you. It's what I do."

"You'll be over a hundred when I'm eighty."

"Yeah. I'll be a hundred and four. What's your point? An old woman can't worry about her daughter? I'll still be a fox at that age, by the way."

"Yeah. Okay. And I'm sure all the other old women will be chasing you."

But there was only one Hannah hoped would catch her. Maggie. All she had to do was stop running. And she had done that. But Maggie didn't catch her because Maggie didn't want her anymore.

"Mom, you seem a million miles away," Cassidy said.

"I'm sorry. I was just thinking."

"About what?"

"Nothing."

"Don't do that, Mom. We've had enough secrets that have caused enough problems. If you don't want to tell me, that's one thing. But don't say it's nothing when obviously that's not the truth."

Hannah had to admit that Cassidy had a point. She wasn't ready to tell her everything going through her head, but she could share some of it. "I was just thinking how sorry I am for pushing Maggie away and blaming her for you getting hurt."

"Did you tell her that?"

"I did."

Cassidy seemed to relax into her seat. "So, everything's going to be all right."

I sure hope so, Hannah thought. I sure hope so.

❖

Maggie had been thinking about Hannah's apology for the last several days. She believed she was sincere but had no idea of her intentions beyond that. Of course, Maggie hadn't given her a chance to say much of anything.

She still wanted Hannah back. Wanted things to be like they were before Cassidy got hurt. But she knew things could never be the same. If they were going to get through this and somehow be together, she knew they would have to have a whole new level of trust. A level they obviously hadn't achieved before.

Her thoughts were interrupted by a knock on the front door. She didn't have any lessons today and Randi was already in the barn working. Besides, Randi wouldn't knock, she would just stick her head in the back door and call to her.

She set her cup of tea on the table and went to the front door. A large bouquet of flowers greeted her.

"Delivery, ma'am. Where would you like these?" The man holding the flowers tilted them to the side just enough that Maggie could see his face.

"Um. I'll take them. Hold on. I'll get you a tip." She took the flowers and started to the kitchen to get her wallet.

"Wait. There's more for you in the truck and I was given strict orders not to accept any money. A very generous tip was provided by the sender." He returned to his truck and brought back two more bouquets. One roses. Lots and lots of red roses, with one yellow one right in the center.

"Holy cow. That's a lot of flowers," Maggie said. She stepped back to let the delivery guy pass. "Could you just set them on the coffee table?"

"Not done yet," he said. "One more trip."

"Seriously?"

He didn't respond but came back with two more good-size bouquets and one smaller one. "I believe there is a card on this one," he said, handing it to her. He put the other two with the rest on the coffee table.

Maggie thanked him.

"Someone must really like you," he said and closed the door behind him.

Maggie just stood and stared at all the flowers for several long moments before she remembered there was a card. She found it tucked in between the daisies and pink baby's breath. She didn't even know baby's breath came in that color.

The card was handwritten in black pen. Maggie read it out loud. "*I truly am sorry. H.*"

She jumped when there was another knock on the door. "More?" she said as she opened it.

"More what?" It was Hannah, holding a cardboard box. "I heard you had some flowers that might need vases." She held the box up higher. "I brought you a few. Can I come in?"

"Um, yes." Maggie stepped back. "Yes, of course."

"Wow," Hannah said, setting the box down on the floor. "That's a lot of flowers." She smiled.

Oh, how Maggie had missed that smile. "It is. It must have cost a fortune," Maggie said.

"I've got connections." That smile again. "Can we talk?" She reached out for Maggie's hand.

Maggie let her take it. She never knew someone holding her hand could feel so good. But this wasn't just anyone. It was Hannah.

Hannah led her to the couch and they sat, leaving some space between them. Too much space. Maggie searched Hannah's face for some clue to how she was feeling and what she was about to say.

Hannah started. "I already said I'm sorry. And I want you to know I meant it. What I failed to say was…" She hesitated. "Was I want you back. I want us to be together. I've missed you. Really, really missed you. I know we disagreed on the whole jumping thing and I made such a big deal of it." Her eyes filled with tears and she looked away.

Maggie gently cupped Hannah's chin, bringing her face back toward her, and looked into her eyes. "It's okay. We can disagree and I can admit when you're wrong."

Hannah laughed. The tears that had been filling her eyes escaped down her cheeks.

Maggie wiped them away. "You're laughing and crying at the same time?"

"See what you do to me? Up is down. Down is up. I laugh. I cry. I make an ass of myself and I beg you to forgive me."

"Beg?"

Hannah laughed again. "Yes. I beg with flowers. It's what I do. You know how important flowers are to me. I wanted to show you how important *you* are to me. Because you are, Maggie. You are so important to me." She intertwined her fingers with Maggie's. "An answer would be nice here."

Maggie felt the need to make her wonder, just a bit longer. "What was the question?"

"Really? You're going to do this to me?"

"Apparently."

"Okay. The question is—will you forgive me and give me—give us—another chance?"

Maggie leaned over and gave Hannah a kiss on the mouth. A long, hard, kiss on the mouth.

"Is that a yes? Oh, please let that be a yes."

"Do you think I kiss just anyone like that?" Maggie asked.

"Oh God, I hope not."

"That's a yes."

"I've missed you," Hannah said again.

"I've missed you, too. And Milkshake has been asking about you. I didn't know what to tell him."

"You can tell him I'm back and that I have been a horse's ass." She scrunched up her face. "Although he might find that offensive. Huh?"

Maggie held her hand up with her thumb and finger close together. "A little bit. Yeah."

"Even though it still scares me a little—or a little more than a little—I would like to go for another ride on the trail. With you."

She smiled. "In fact, there's lots of things I would like to do with you. And to you." A blush creeped up her neck to her cheeks.

"Right back 'atcha. Know what I'm thinking we should do right now?" Maggie asked.

"Does it involve your bedroom and little to no clothes?"

"Not even close."

Hannah pouted. "Damn."

"No. I think we need to put all of these flowers in water. And seeing as you have a box full of vases there…" She pointed to the box on the floor. "You can help me." She stood and pulled Hannah up with her. "And then we can go do something involving little to no clothes."

"It's a deal." Hannah pulled Maggie into a tight hug. "I know it's really soon, but I need to tell you that I think I'm falling in love with you." She kissed her gently on the lips, pulled back, and looked into her eyes. "And by think, I mean I know. And by falling, I mean I already fell." She kissed her again. "What I am trying to say is I love you."

Maggie had felt love too but had kept it tucked away deep in her heart, afraid that it would hurt too much if she was in love alone. But she wasn't alone in this. Hannah was right here with her. In her arms. "I love you too."

"So, where do we go from here?" Hannah asked.

"Flowers. Water. Bedroom. Little to no clothes. Expanding. Lots and lots of expanding."

EPILOGUE

Y ou need to put the blindfold on," Hannah told Maggie. Maggie wasn't so sure about this. She wasn't sure why her not being able to see was necessary.

"Trust me on this. Have I ever steered you wrong?"

"Well, there was that one time you told me to try Hunan spicy beef. It will be fun, you said. You're gonna love it, you said. I thought my mouth was on fire. Remember that?"

Hannah laughed. "Forget that. I promise this will be fun and you won't burn your tongue."

"But why do I have to be blindfolded?" Maggie asked.

"Because I don't want you to see anything. I'll be right there with you the whole time. You're not alone. I won't leave you even for a second. We're doing this together."

"But I'm the only one with the blindfold on."

"One of us has to be able to see what we're doing, silly girl."

"Are you sure about this? I mean, I'm all up for adventure. But this—" She held up the blindfold. "Might be taking it a bit too far."

Hannah raised her eyebrows. "Honey, please."

"I hate it when you beg," Maggie said.

"Oh, I know that's not true. Just the other night—"

"Okay. Okay. I'll put it on. But you better have a hold on me the whole time."

"I promise."

Maggie put the blindfold on and tied it in the back. Her world went dark, and she felt a slight breeze in front of her face. "Did you just run your hands over my eyes to make sure I can't see?"

"Can you?"

"Did you?"

"Yep. Can you see?" Hannah asked.

"I don't think I'm liking this game. No. I can't see a thing."

"Good." Hannah started the car and pulled it out onto the street.

It felt like she turned left out of the driveway. Maggie tried to guess where they were going but gave up after the third turn.

"Here we are," Hannah exclaimed as she turned the car off. "Unbuckle and I'll come around and get you."

Maggie heard her door open, and Hannah took her arm to help her out of the car. Hannah kept one arm wrapped around Maggie's waist as she guided her.

"Wait. I need to open the door."

Maggie stopped.

"Okay. Forward. Two steps—up—good. Now we just go straight."

"Can I take this off now?" Maggie put her hand on the blindfold.

"Not yet."

Hannah led her down what seemed like a long hallway. Another pause while Hannah opened another door and she was guided inside.

"Okay. You can take it off."

"Surprise!" a chorus of people yelled. There was Cassidy, home from veterinary college, her sister, Jean; oh, and her dad. She was surrounded by her family, Hannah's family, and their friends. She looked up. The banner against the wall read *Happy 50th Anniversary*. She looked at Hannah with a question in her eyes.

"You told me early on that you wanted to be able to celebrate your fiftieth wedding anniversary with the person you love. I know this is only our fifth anniversary, but, honey, I want to give you everything you ever wanted."

Maggie wiped the tears that filled her eyes and made a trail down her cheeks. "I have everything I've ever wanted. I love you."

Hannah kissed her. "I love you too."

About the Author

Creativity for Joy Argento started young. She was only five, growing up in Syracuse, New York, when she picked up a pencil and began drawing animals. These days she calls Rochester home, and oil paints are her medium of choice. Her award-winning art has found its way into homes around the globe.

Writing came later in life for Joy. Her love of lesbian romance inspired her to try her hand at writing, and she found her first self-published novels well received. She is thrilled to be a part of the Bold Strokes family and has enjoyed their books for years.

Joy has three grown children who are making their own way in the world and five grandsons who are the light of her life.

Books Available from Bold Strokes Books

A Fox in Shadow by Jane Fletcher. Cassie's mission is to add new territory to the Kavillian empire—murder, betrayal, war, and the clash of cultures ensue. (978-1-63679-142-5)

Embracing the Moon by Jeannie Levig. Just as Gwen and Taylor are exploring the new love they've found, the present and past collide, threatening the future they long to share. (978-1-63555-462-5)

Forever Comes in Threes by D. Jackson Leigh. Efficiency expert Perry Chandler's ordered life is upended when she inherits three busy terriers, and the woman she's referred to for help turns out to be her bitter podcast rival, the very sexy Dr. Ming Lee. (978-1-63679-169-2)

Heckin' Lewd: Trans and Nonbinary Erotica by Mx. Nillin Lore. If you want smutty, fearless, gender diverse erotica written by affirming own-voices folks who get it, then this is the book you've been looking for! (978-1-63679-240-8)

Missed Conception by Joy Argento. Maggie Walsh wants a relationship with Cassidy, the daughter she's only just discovered she has due to an in vitro mix-up. Heat kindles between Maggie and Cassidy's mother in a way neither expects. (978-1-63679-146-3)

Private Equity by Elle Spencer. Cassidy Bennett spends an unexpected evening at a lesbian nightclub with her notoriously reserved and demanding boss, Julia. After seeing a different side of Julia, Cassidy can't seem to shake her desire to know more. (978-1-63679-180-7)

Racing the Dawn by Sandra Barrett. After narrowly escaping a house fire, vampire Jade Murphy is unexpectedly intrigued by gorgeous firefighter Beth Jenssen, and her undead existence might just be perking up a bit. (978-1-63679-271-2)

Reclaiming Love by Amanda Radley. Sarah's tiny white lie means somehow convincing Pippa to pretend to be her girlfriend. Only the more time they spend faking it, the more real it feels. (978-1-63679-144-9)

Sol Cycle by Kimberly Cooper Griffin. An encounter in a park brings Ang and Krista together, but when Ang's attempts to help Krista go spectacularly wrong, their passion for each other might not be enough. (978-1-63679-137-1)

Trial and Error by Carsen Taite. Attorney Franco Rossi and Judge Nina Aguilar's reunion is fraught with courtroom conflict, undeniable chemistry, and danger. (978-1-63555-863-0)

A Long Way to Fall by Elle Spencer. A ski lodge, two strong-willed women, and a family feud that brings them together, but will it also tear them apart? (978-1-63679-005-3)

Barnabas Bopwright Saves the City by J. Marshall Freeman. When he uncovers a terror plot to destroy the city he loves, 15-year-old Barnabas Bopwright realizes it's up to him to save his home and bring deadly secrets into the light before it's too late. (978-1-63679-152-4)

Forever by Kris Bryant. When Savannah Edwards is invited to be the next bachelorette on the dating show When Sparks Fly, she'll show the world that finding true love on television can happen. (978-1-63679-029-9)

Ice on Wheels by Aurora Rey. All's fair in love and roller derby. That's Riley Fauchet's motto, until a new job lands her at the same company—and on the same team—as her rival Brooke Landry, the frosty jammer for the Big Easy Bruisers. (978-1-63679-179-1)

Inherit the Lightning by Bud Gundy. Darcy O'Brien and his sisters learn they are about to inherit an immense fortune, but a family mystery about to unravel after seventy years threatens to destroy everything. (978-1-63679-199-9)

Perfect Rivalry by Radclyffe. Two women set out to win the same career-making goal, but it's love that may turn out to be the final prize. (978-1-63679-216-3)

Something to Talk About by Ronica Black. Can quiet ranch owner Corey Durand give up her peaceful life and allow her feisty new neighbor into her heart? Or will past loss, present suitors, and town gossip ruin a long-awaited chance at love? (978-1-63679-114-2)

With a Minor in Murder by Karis Walsh. In the world of academia, police officer Clare Sawyer and professor Libby Hart team up to solve a murder. (978-1-63679-186-9)

Writer's Block by Ali Vali. Wyatt and Hayley might be made for each other if only they can get through nosy neighbors, the historic society, at-odds future plans, and all the secrets hidden in Wyatt's walls. (978-1-63679-021-3)

Cold Blood by Genevieve McCluer. Maybe together, Kalila and Dorenia have a chance of taking down the vampires who have eluded them all these years. And maybe, in each other, they can find a love worth living for. (978-1-63679-195-1)

Greener Pastures by Aurora Rey. When city girl and CPA Audrey Adams finds herself tending her aunt's farm, will Rowan Marshall—the charming cider maker next door—turn out to be her saving grace or the bane of her existence? (978-1-63679-116-6)

Grounded by Amanda Radley. For a second chance, Olivia and Emily will need to accept their mistakes, learn to communicate properly, and with a little help from five-year-old Henry, fall madly in love all over again. Sequel to Flight SQA016. (978-1-63679-241-5)

Journey's End by Amanda Radley. In this heartwarming conclusion to the Flight series, Olivia and Emily must finally decide what they want, what they need, and how to follow the dreams of their hearts. (978-1-63679-233-0)

Pursued: Lillian's Story by Felice Picano. Fleeing a disastrous marriage to the Lord Exchequer of England, Lillian of Ravenglass reveals an incident-filled, often bizarre, tale of great wealth and power, perfidy, and betrayal. (978-1-63679-197-5)

Secret Agent by Michelle Larkin. CIA agent Peyton North embarks on a global chase to apprehend rogue agent Zoey Blackwood, but her commitment to the mission is tested as the sparks between them ignite and their sizzling attraction approaches a point of no return. (978-1-63555-753-4)

Something Between Us by Krystina Rivers. A decade after her heart was broken under Don't Ask, Don't Tell, Kirby runs into her first love and has to decide if what's still between them is enough to heal her broken heart. (978-1-63679-135-7)

Sugar Girl by Emma L McGeown. Having traded in traditional romance for the perks of Sugar Dating, Ciara Reilly not only enjoys the no-strings-attached arrangement, she's also a hit with her clients. That is until she meets the beautiful entrepreneur Charlie Keller who makes her want to go sugar-free. (978-1-63679-156-2)

The Business of Pleasure by Ronica Black. Editor in chief Valerie Raffield is quickly becoming smitten by Lennox, the graphic artist she's hired to work remotely. But when Lennox doesn't show for their first face-to-face meeting, Valerie's heart and her business may be in jeopardy. (978-1-63679-134-0)

The Hummingbird Sanctuary by Erin Zak. The Hummingbird Sanctuary, Colorado's hottest resort destination: Come for the mountains, stay for the charm, and enjoy the drama as Olive, Eleanor, and Harriet figure out the meaning of true friendship. (978-1-63679-163-0)

The Witch Queen's Mate by Jennifer Karter. Barra and Silvi must overcome their ingrained hatred and prejudice to use Barra's magic and save both their peoples, not just from slavery, but destruction. (978-1-63679-202-6)

With a Twist by Georgia Beers. Starting over isn't easy for Amelia Martini. When the irritatingly cheerful Kirby Dupress comes into her life will Amelia be brave enough to go after the love she really wants? (978-1-63555-987-3)

Business of the Heart by Claire Forsythe. When a hopeless romantic meets a tough-as-nails cynic, they'll need to overcome the wounds of the past to discover that their hearts are the most important business of all. (978-1-63679-167-8)

Dying for You by Jenny Frame. Can Victorija Dred keep an age-old vow and fight the need to take blood from Daisy Macdougall? (978-1-63679-073-2)

Exclusive by Melissa Brayden. Skylar Ruiz lands the TV reporting job of a lifetime, but is she willing to sacrifice it all for the love of her longtime crush, anchorwoman Carolyn McNamara? (978-1-63679-112-8)

Her Duchess to Desire by Jane Walsh. An up-and-coming interior designer seeks to create a happily ever after with an intriguing duchess, proving that love never goes out of fashion. (978-1-63679-065-7)

Murder on Monte Vista by David S. Pederson. Private Detective Mason Adler's angst at turning fifty is forgotten when his "birthday present," the handsome, young Henry Bowtrickle, turns up dead, and it's up to Mason to figure out who did it, and why. (978-1-63679-124-1)

Take Her Down by Lauren Emily Whalen. Stakes are cutthroat, scheming is creative, and loyalty is ever-changing in this queer, female-driven YA retelling of Shakespeare's Julius Caesar. (978-1-63679-089-3)

The Game by Jan Gayle. Ryan Gibbs is a talented golfer, but her guilt means she may never leave her small town, even if Katherine Reese tempts her with competition and passion. (978-1-63679-126-5)

Whereabouts Unknown by Meredith Doench. While homicide detective Theodora Madsen recovers from a potentially career-ending injury, she scrambles to solve the cases of two missing sixteen-year-old girls from Ohio. (978-1-63555-647-6)

Boy at the Window by Lauren Melissa Ellzey. Daniel Kim struggles to hold onto reality while haunted by both his very-present past and his never-present parents. Jiwon Yoon may be the only one who can break Daniel free. (978-1-63679-092-3)

Deadly Secrets by VK Powell. Corporate criminals want whistleblower Jana Elliott permanently silenced, but Rafe Silva will risk everything to keep the woman she loves safe. (978-1-63679-087-9)

Enchanted Autumn by Ursula Klein. When Elizabeth comes to Salem, Massachusetts, to study the witch trials, she never expects to find love—or an actual witch…and Hazel might just turn out to be both. (978-1-63679-104-3)

Escorted by Renee Roman. When fantasy meets reality, will escort Ryan Lewis be able to walk away from a chance at forever with her new client Dani? (978-1-63679-039-8)

Her Heart's Desire by Anne Shade. Two women. One choice. Will Eve and Lynette be able to overcome their doubts and fears to embrace their deepest desire? (978-1-63679-102-9)

My Secret Valentine by Julie Cannon, Erin Dutton, & Anne Shade. Winning the heart of your secret Valentine? These award-winning authors agree, there is no better way to fall in love. (978-1-63679-071-8)

Perilous Obsession by Carsen Taite. When reporter Macy Moran becomes consumed with solving a cold case, will her quest for the truth bring her closer to Detective Beck Ramsey or will her obsession with finding a murderer rob her of a chance at true love? (978-1-63679-009-1)

Reading Her by Amanda Radley. Lauren and Allegra learn love and happiness are right where they least expect it. There's just one problem: Lauren has a secret she cannot tell anyone, and Allegra knows she's hiding something. (978-1-63679-075-6)

The Willing by Lyn Hemphill. Kitty Wilson doesn't know how, but she can bring people back from the dead as long as someone is willing to take their place and keep the universe in balance. (978-1-63679-083-1)

Three Left Turns to Nowhere by Nathan Burgoine, J. Marshall Freeman, & Jeffrey Ricker. Three strangers heading to a convention in Toronto are stranded in rural Ontario, where a small town with a subtle kind of magic leads each to discover what he's been searching for. (978-1-63679-050-3)

Watching Over Her by Ronica Black. As they face the snowstorm of the century, and the looming threat of a stalker, Riley and Zoey just might find love in the most unexpected of places. (978-1-63679-100-5)